Sorry, Charlie

For Bon Bon.

August 27, Sunday

Kathy Wheels: This is Kathy Wheels reporting live at 1114 LaTrace, here on Lake Cleburne. We can't actually get down the driveway to the cabin at this point, but we have seen a few interesting things. For instance, there's the SUV, a Jimmy, that was pulled from the waters of the lake early this morning. When it passed by us here on the wrecker, we noticed what looked like possible bullet holes in the windows and roof. That may or may not be the case.

Then there's the cell phone, which one of our camera guys actually found before the police. It was right over here, Martin [Kathy walks over to a spot in the road where there appears to be a slight indentation. Camera zooms to empty hole.] where we found a cell phone that looked like it had been submerged in some sort of acid solution. Very strange stuff Martin.

Martin Langley: And the dogs, Kathy? There seems to be a link between the numerous dogs found on the property and the vandalism at the Pet Cemetery not far from there? Is that correct?

Kathy Wheels: That has not been confirmed yet. However, yesterday at Pine Crest Cemetery there was already an investigation underway concerning well over a hundred animals that had been dug up the night before. A reliable source has told us that there are dead dogs scattered all over the property behind us, just down the driveway here. They are apparently in the house, and Martin, even, our source assures us, in the attic where Daniel Stauberg was also found yesterday evening by his ex-wife and her companion in the early morning hours.

A couple of more strange things, Martin. They said the house was completely flooded and that piles of junk were everywhere, similar to barricades.

Martin Langley: And Daniel, the man that was, uh, found torn to pieces in the attic. What information do we have on him, Kathy?

Kathy Wheels: In a very confused and emotional statement we have from his ex-wife, we found out that they were going through a divorce and that she believed he was responsible for the death of her dog. Let's see [shuffles some papers in her hands] . . . Charlie, who has not yet been accounted for on the property. That info from Ben Braswell on the PD, meaning that his wife wasn't able to identify any of the animals as hers. And there were apparently quite a few liquor bottles found empty, Martin.

Martin Langley: Well, Kathy . . . divorce can be a stressful event. Did they say exactly how Daniel died?

Kathy Wheels: Oh, here comes officer Braswell. Sir! Officer Braswell! [Kathy runs up to the cruiser and shoves the mic in Ben Braswell's face.] Can you tell us anything new, Officer Braswell?

Ben Braswell: Well, Kathy. It looks like Daniel Stauberg was going through a really rough time and just snapped. It appears that some of the dogs he drug up here were still alive and attacked and killed him.

Kathy Wheels: In the attic? [With an air of disbelief.]

Ben Braswell: Well . . . yeah. It looks like he drug a good many up to the attic and then threw them out the attic vent. Just a huge pile of dead animals piled up against the house. Very disturbing behavior. But with all the liquor bottles we found, anything's possible.

Kathy Wheels: Thank you, Officer. [Officer Braswell drives away.] Back to you Martin.

Martin Langley: Thanks, Kathy. In another strange story, it seems birds are falling from the skies again, but this time it's not just a few thousand. We go to Rob Williams, live in Ridley, AL. Rob.

August 25, Friday

"A place?"

There was another pause, this one longer and somehow more pronounced. The silence had a weight to it that pressed against his stomach, and then the back of his eyeballs. The car behind him beeped its horn. He had a headache. Dan the Man, as his drinking buddies called him, started turning things over and over in only the way that a "Dan the Man" could. For one, what in the hell had come over her? It had to be that bitch Carol she was shacked up with for the moment. He could see her working against him every step of the way. For two, how the hell did she think she was going to make it financially on her own? That was ridiculous.

"Yes, a place."

It was a sad "yes," but he detected a firmness in it that he really didn't appreciate. It just wasn't like her. She was being contrary and doing so over the phone where he couldn't sit her down and straighten her out.

"That's ridiculous. Just come back to the *damn* house would ya, so we can talk this out?"

The car behind Dan beeped its horn again, and Dan jerked the Jimmy forward.

And then a string of words hit Dan's ears that he really didn't know how to respond to.

"I'm not coming back in that *FUCKING* house where you had that little *BITCH* of yours! Are you that *FUCKING* dense!"

The phone clicked and Dan slammed on the brakes, just missing the truck's rear bumper that was idling at the four-way stop in front of him. About the time he was going to transition from shocked to pissed, there was a squealing sound, the kind rubber makes when trying to grab asphalt, and he flew forward against the steering wheel.

He stumbled out of the car, a trail of disbelief and confusion following him. Just a week ago, life was good. Things were in order. The planets were aligned. And now it was like the whole fucking universe was working against him.

The hit from behind sent his Jimmy a few feet forward and crashing into the back of an old Ford truck. A rusty grunt of a man crawled from the truck. A week-old beard obscured a haggard face and a cigarette hung from the corner of his mouth. He looked at Dan and Dan looked at him. Dan could only throw his hands up. The old man moseyed past him and looked at the small dent that was on his back bumper. About as big around as a quarter and no deeper than a centimeter. There was a tiny smudge of black paint from the front of Dan's SUV. Dan looked at his left headlight assembly. Part of it was still on the Jimmy and the other part was strewn across the pavement.

Dan knew the rules. You hit someone from behind and it was your fault. Period. So he turned toward the oversized Cadillac behind him. A small lady, who looked to be in her eighties, was slowly rocking back and forth, gathering enough momentum to roll out of her driver's seat. The squeals of a small Chihuahua, from somewhere inside the urban monstrosity, became muffled as she finally shut the door. She stopped. Pressed her glasses into a firm position on her nose and locked eyes with Dan.

"You were on the phone!" she hollered, as loud as an eighty-something-year-old woman can yell. The white-haired woman's words were accusatory and laced with contempt. She then looked to the curb at the few people gathering there between Moe's and the Jewelry shop. "Did anyone see this man on the phone?" she asked the crowd as a whole.

Dan was still in disbelief. This lady rammed into him, and here she was trying to get him into more trouble. He turned to flash his incredulous smile to the crowd and saw a guy in jeans and a button-down white shirt gingerly and slowly raise his hand.

Dan knew the rules on this as well. A new ordinance passed by some crazy-ass parents. No texting while driving. And although he wasn't texting, he didn't like being accused of anything period. And Karen's words were still ringing in his ears.

"*Are you that fucking dense?*"

"This is ridiculous!" he exclaimed to no one in particular. No one seemed to be listening. A few people were actually headed in the old lady's direction as she began preaching to everyone in earshot about the evils of driving while on the phone. Dan couldn't stop shaking his head. This was unreal.

He looked back at the old man who was staring at the older woman with a trace of a smile forming around his cigarette. It was as if he were watching two cows do it in the pasture. Just a funny little thing that happened on the way home. That's all. And why should he care? Dan thought. You can't even hardly tell I hit his truck. Now I'm looking at a new head light assembly.

Then the flashing red and blue lights pulled up to the side of all three cars, in effect, blocking traffic. Why do they always do that? Dan thought to himself. They could pull out of the damn road, but no, they always park right in the middle of it.

As the officer crawled out of his cruiser, Dan could see the bored reserve on his face. Just another shitty workday. This should be fun. The old lady made a beeline for the cop, her new-found pansy friend trailing uncertainly behind, a safe distance from drama should it ensue.

"This one was on the phone!" she began telling him. "He'd been waving his hands around in that thing with it glued to his ear for the last five minutes, all the way from Sutton. Just ask anybody."

"Yes, mam." The cop looked unimpressed, even irritated. Maybe that was a good thing. He could talk sense to the cop.

"I need everybody's licenses, registration, and proof of insurance. Is anyone harmed?" The cop started filling out some form and never looked up as he asked the question.

"Sir, from the looks of it, I'm the only one with real damage to my vehicle. You can't even tell where I hit the old man's truck, and I don't see any damage to the old lady's Caddy either. Is there any way we can just wrap this up? It's Friday."

The cop raised his eyebrows and stared at Dan with a poker face. Then he turned to the old man, leaning on the front of Dan's Jimmy like he owned it and still puffing nonchalantly away on his cigarette. The old man shrugged as an answer. The cop turned to the old lady, and she just stared back, oblivious to the deal being brokered. The cop looked exasperated.

"The fellow here says there's no damage to anyone's vehicle but his. If that's true and you don't mind, then we don't have to fill out a report. Is this okay with you mam?"

Everyone was looking at the old lady. She looked around, momentarily taken aback by the fact that the ball was in her court. She looked at the front of her car, as did the cop and Dan, the old man scanning the crowd and smiling. Then she raised her head pridefully, obstinately.

"I want a report." The cop sighed and returned to filling out the form on his clipboard. "I want this to be an example to all the people who want to talk on their phones while they should be driving. I had a nephew in Pendergrass that was yapping on one of those things, and it wasn't a few weeks until he ran up on a curb and took out a newspaper vending machine. Coulda been someone's child. If they woulda had this ordinance . . ."

"This is complete bullshit," Dan said loud enough for everyone to hear. The cop looked up from his clipboard.

"License, registration, and proof of insurance, sir." It wasn't a request.

Dan walked back to his SUV and plopped down in the seat. Out of his passenger's window, he watched as traffic slowly rerouted itself around the cars. Faces stared at them as if they were on display. Some curious circus creatures. Dan was on stage, but not in a good way. He popped open the glove compartment. It took him five minutes to find the registration and insurance envelop. He walked back to show the cop and had to wait for what seemed like ten minutes on the old lady and geezer who were now in front of him.

The cop finally took the papers and handed his license and registration back. He waved the insurance papers in front of Dan.

"This expired last month," the cop said.

Dan stared dumbly back for a moment. "Yes, sir. My wife handles all that stuff. I'm sure it's at the house or in her purse or something."

"You don't have it on you?

"No sir."

"I can get it to someone on Monday, if that's alright."

"Can't let you drive the vehicle without proof of insurance, sir." The cop's pen kept scratching indifferently at the paper.

Dan was in disbelief. Arguing with cops never turned out good. He knew that much. He steamed silently for a moment as the cop continued to ignored him.

Then it hit him that he couldn't call his wife to ask her where it was because said wife had essentially told him to go fuck himself. Un-fucking-believable. Just wonderful. Dan was so pissed that, at first, he couldn't even think to call the number on the insurance paper to get the information. When he did, as he was listening to it ring, he realized that no one was going to answer because it was past five o'clock.

He let it ring and ring out of desperation, and after twenty or so rings, the guy who sold them the insurance a couple of years ago answered. Dan explained his situation and, after doing a little begging, got him to print the papers out and run them twenty minutes across town to him in the middle of the street.

"Make sure you get the headlight fixed as soon as possible," was the only thing the cop had to offer before leaving.

Dan drove home in a state of simmering anger and fizzling energy. He walked in and sat on the couch, exhausted. Stared at the black screen on the TV for five minutes as he replayed the last hour in his head. Over and over again. Then he got up and grabbed a beer.

Another expense. Another unjustified pain-in-the-ass expense. He sat in his chair and thought, not about his wife or the car, but about Sheryl. Sheryl's tight ass, willingness to please, and flirty little eyes that beckoned you to throw her on the table and take her from behind, even when you were just having a normal conversation. And that's just what had happened over a week ago right in the living room.

It was a spur of the moment thing, nothing you could really blame either of them for, and then Karen walked through the door an hour early from work and found her husband of one year dick-deep in a friend from work. For a second, Dan the Man had actually thought that maybe he could work it for the good; after all, wasn't this the way the stories always started in the Penthouse Forum.

But this story goes another direction. Karen screamed at them while he tried to use one of their pillows to cover up his messy privates. He couldn't follow her past the front door with his pants around his ankles.

After that, Sheryl wanted to go home immediately. The ride was awkward, and all he could manage was "I'm sorry for all that," and "I'll see you tomorrow," neither of which Sheryl seemed to take the right way. Then she managed to avoid him the whole of last week. He hadn't even nutted that day. It wasn't fair. This was *bullshit.*

And now he had a crunched front bumper and no left-side headlight, which all the neighbors could surely see from the street. There was no telling what Karen was saying to their shared circle of friends to make him look like a shmuck.

Dan the Man picked up the phone to call Parker and then hung it up. He didn't want to have to be answering all kinds of questions about this stupid, stupid *bullshit.*

He got up and got another beer from the fridge. The first six were the best. The chilled barley and hops numbed his mind to the external world. To things that didn't make sense. His mind stayed on the witty comments from Patricia Heaton and then the young shirtless women from his Girls Gone Wild collection.

That's when the real nasty thoughts started pouring in. They ranged from the things he'd like to do to Sheryl while Karen watched, to things he'd like for Karen to do to him while Sheryl watched. Then he was beating the shit out of the arrogant cop who wrote up the accident report. Then he was tying up the crazy old bitch, who had wrecked his car and throwing her down from the overpass onto the cars below. The whole world, by beer number ten, could kiss his hairy ass.

It was during the consumption of the tenth beer that Daniel Stauberg began having rather evil thoughts about Charlie. Who the *fuck* did ole Charlie think he was anyway? This was *his* house. *His* backyard. And what business did some hairy mutt of a shit-layin' factory have growling at him in his own damn yard?

First, there was Go-Lite; some kind of stuff the doctor used to clean you out before surgery. That would teach the little turd layer a thing or two. He wouldn't take a number two, he would take a number three. He would put him on the run in the back yard and stand on the back deck, laughing his ass off while Charlie drug himself along in a permanent hunch.

Then there was the BB gun. That wouldn't penetrate the skin or leave marks that Karen could see. They would just sting a little and really, really piss him off. That would be uber fun.

Beer number eleven.

Beer number eleven eased Dan the Man into a slight depression, following on the heels of an angry-at-the-whole-world spell. Karen had gotten over on him. Her best friend was probably working to get her laid right now. The shithead cop was probably laughing with his buddies about the dumbass he met today. The old lady that creamed her piece of shit car into his was probably whining to her old fart of a husband, if he hadn't already keeled over. And the dog was just waiting to take a chunk of the hand that fed it.

Beer twelve.

The only thing that was on the tube now was infomercials and B movies with the worst of the eighties actors. What ever happened to the *A-Team* or *Mork and Mindy?*

Beer thirteen.

Three piss breaks with little or no detectable brain activity.

Then, beer fourteen. The twelve pack of South Paw was gone, and the last two beers he would force down were Karen's nasty little Corona's. *Nice commercials with shitty beer,* he thought, swallowing another gulp with a wince.

The BB gun it is. Dan got up and staggered immediately to his left and fell over the footstool.

"Shit!"

Now he wore a little imported perfume on his chest and arm. He gained his feet and made his way to the back door. The BB gun was lying next to the pellet gun in a pile of junk in the corner. He lifted a baseball bat and horseshoe off the gun and stumbled towards the door. He looked out into the dimly lit backyard.

It was a decent size spread for the little squat of suburbia they had purchased over a year ago. A few trees for shade, which seemed to be disappearing from yards as a trend, and a nice combo shed that he could pull his boat in to keep out of the weather. There was a homemade doghouse sitting next to the back corner of the shed. It *looked* homemade.

From the corner of the shed above the shanty, there was a red line that ran across the yard catty-cornered, about four feet off the ground, to one of the shade trees. He would have to lure the dog to his tie-on before he could have his fun. He weaved his way to the pisser, hit the lid, splattered his leg, stumbled to the fridge, grabbed some ham, made his way by the junk drawer, and picked up a Phillips Head screwdriver then walked out the back door.

"Heeeere shithead!"

A chicken was being roasted in just under twenty minutes on the TV as he called for Charlie. He stood on his tip toes and peered over the fence to make sure that no backyard lights were on in the neighbor's yard.

Dan caught a glimpse from the corner of his eye and jumped a little. The dog had appeared from the shadows to his left and stopped short of Dan. Charlie stood stolid as a soldier and stared at Dan. He hated that stare. It was a challenge and Dan knew it. It was a staring contest.

Dan's grip tightened on the screwdriver as he flung his other arm out and let go of a couple of slices of honey ham. The dog looked down at the ham, back up at Dan, and then bent down and swallowed the two pieces without chewing. Charlie looked up at Dan again, eager to resume the staring contest.

Dan wanted to just stab the dog and show the sonofabitch who was in charge, but after stumbling around the house for the past ten minutes, Dan wasn't feeling quite like the man anymore. He walked towards the run where the tie-on was dangling at the far end. Charlie followed slowly behind.

When they reached the tie-on, Dan grabbed it in one hand and held the ham in the other. Now came the tricky part. The clasp on the run was easy, and Dan already had it slid open with his thumb. The problem was getting it attached to the silver ring on the collar, the part that was close to the jaws. If he dropped the ham and tried to use both hands, Charlie might think he was attempting to grab the food and snap at him. He would have to feed him with the left hand and feel for the ring with the other, snapping it on while leaning on one knee so he wouldn't fall flat on his face. Charlie was stopped about four feet away and was looking back and forth, between Dan and the remaining ham. His head stayed locked in the same position. Only Charlie's eyes moved.

The staring contest was now being interrupted by Charlie's hunger. It had been a day and a half since Dan had fed him. A few uncomfortable seconds passed and, for a moment, Dan thought Charlie wasn't going to move. Then Charlie seemed to ease up a little and moved forward to the ham.

Dan moved with the precision and quickness of a surgeon; and so did Charlie.

At the same time that Dan felt the loop and let go of the snap, Charlie swallowed the ham and turned on Dan. Dan moved backward as quickly as someone squatting can, and fell over backwards. He then rolled over, much like the cops did in the 80's B movies when dodging bullets, and was on his shaky legs in no time.

Charlie's snapping teeth and guttural attack was over with as quickly as it started. Charlie stood his ground and immediately began another staring contest with Dan.

Dan's heart thumped in his chest until he thought it would surely rattle loose and start pinballing its way amongst his internal organs. He stared back in disbelief. Charlie was hooked to the line. Good. Dan was covered in dirt and grass and suddenly felt a tight pressure in the bladder area.

"Stupid, Shit!" he screamed at the dog as he lifted up on shaky legs back to the house.

Moving quickly to the bathroom, Dan began to notice a nasty stench. Flicking on the bathroom light, he saw the culprit. Smeared on his side, like he was a PB&J in the making, was a pasty gift from Charlie that Dan had rolled over in the yard.

"Nice! That's just nice!" Dan yelled at no one in particular. He would have to shower now. He unzipped his pants and looked down to aim. Aside from Karen cussing him today, this was the only thing that would have left him totally speechless. There was a slight tear on his right hand, just above the thumb and a drizzle of blood ran its way down onto his privates. His bladder exploded, and for the next twenty-five seconds all he could do was stare at the wound, dumbfounded.

Dan crawled into the shower and tightened up when the hot water ran over the tear. He wondered for a minute if it would need stitches. As the dumbfoundedness waned, the anger stepped in. No BB gun now. Now it was the pellet gun.

Charlie broke the skin, so now I'll break the skin.

"He drew first blood, sir," Dan said to an imaginary officer in his best Stallone slur. He giggled a drunken giggle. Let the warm water wash away the stink and blood and then held his head underneath the water until it ran cold. He walked naked to his room and threw on another pair of pants and a dirty T-shirt.

In the back of his mind, he'd never figured on actually being bitten, but with the adrenaline now gone, Dan could feel his hand throbbing with each step to the deck. The pellet gun was pumped, not five, but eleven times. The red line hanging down from the run disappeared into the shadows of the doghouse.

Dan took aim and the concussion sound sent the pellet flying into the darkness, there was a satisfying yelp from within and Charlie bolted from the blackness. He turned and bit at his hindquarter at the embedded steel.

"Hell of a flea bite, huh, sport?" Dan laughed.

Charlie looked up and across the yard at Dan. Dan pumped the rifle up. Another staring contest, huh partner.

He aimed again.

"Let's see who blinks first."

Snap! Another yelp, this one followed by a low growl. Charlie ran half the length of his run and stopped, twirling in circles. He barked once at nothing.

Dan pumped the rifle, with each pressing of the pump he could feel his own wound throb. He took aim again.

Snap! Another yelp. Charlie ran this time, all the way to the end of the run, and got close to the tree.

Snap! Yelp!

Dan laughed. This was going to be fun. Charlie wrapped himself around the tree twice and stopped. He was at rope's end.

Snap! No yelp. This time a growl. Dan looked on from his iron seat while Charlie began to back up. He watched as Charlie's ears and skin bunched up around his collar. The dog pulled and jerked with all its might. Then it was free.

Dan started to wonder what the dog was going to do next when Charlie began running at him full speed. He almost fell getting up and clamored for the door.

When he reached the door, he turned to see where Charlie was only to find him burying his teeth into his leg.

"Aaaagghh!"

This time it was Dan who yelped. It was a pressure he had never experienced and was sure a crocodile had latched onto his leg. He jerked at the door with one hand and dropped the rifle with the other. The dog was blocking the door from opening up enough to slide in. He could feel the teeth sink into his flesh. His stomach suddenly weakened. Then he lost his footing and fell.

Charlie let go and stepped back. Dan should have used the opportunity to escape, but he was in shock. He was supposed to be the one in charge. Instead, he was the one on the ground. Charlie came at him again. Dan managed somehow to move the rifle between the teeth and his head. He could feel the slobber hit his face and could hear the growling, rumbling in his ears.

The dog was on top of him and Dan finally thought to kick. After his tennis shoes met with Charlie's hind leg several times and nothing happened, Dan began to wonder if this was where he would die, in a pool of blood on his own back deck. He kicked one last time - and Charlie let go.

He wasted no time at his second chance and was quickly inside the door. He looked out through the glass to see Charlie staring at him. Looking down at his bloody pants, Dan headed for the bathroom, stopped short, went to the fridge, took out the rest of the ham, grabbed some saran-wrap and his keys on the way out the side door.

He opened the door and threw the ham into the passenger seat. He unrolled the saran wrap and stretched it twenty different ways over his seat. Dan hopped in, hissed through his teeth as his left leg hit the seat, and cranked the vehicle. He hopped back out after dimming the lights to parking only and limped to the fence. He unlatched the gate and cautiously peered in, half expecting Charlie to be crouched down and waiting. There was no sign of him. He swung the fence wide on one side, and then the other. Dan hopped back in, drove through the gate, hopped out and locked the gate back. Then he drove to the middle of the yard and turned off the lights on the SUV.

Rolling down the window, he tossed out the rest of the ham and watched all but a little hit and slide off the front of the hood. He sat back.

The engine idled down quietly.

Dan waited.

Dan awoke, slightly confused at first to his location. As he pushed himself back up from his slumped position, the sharp throbbing pain in his leg and the dull ache in his hand brought him back to his current state. He nervously glanced around, almost sure someone was watching his every move. Nothing.

He heard a noise over the quiet hum of the idling engine. Leaning his head out of the Jimmy's window, he spotted the end of a gray, black furry tail near the left wheel. Applying the break, he pulled the gearshift toward him and the Jimmy shifted a little. The tail disappeared and he knew Charlie had scooted away.

"Dammit, c'mon!" he whispered.

He waited a moment, and still no tail; but Dan could hear the meat smacking in front of the grill. He eased his foot down gently on the accelerator, but not too much. Too much would leave suspicious marks in the grass, marks that Karen might notice when she came to her senses and returned home.

A lurch forward. A loud resounding squeal. A bump-bump-bump. Now more loud squealing. Dan could see his neighbors rushing out of their houses with digital cameras in hand. He saw the cop from yesterday, shaking his head again as he placed the cuffs behind Dan's back.

Turning the wheel quickly, he reversed the car and moved back with less caution. Catching a glimpse of himself in the rearview didn't help matters. He was a sickly pale.

Bump. But not a complete bump-bump. It was like he had rolled on a speed bump, but not fast enough, and had rolled back. He hit the gas. The wheels slipped for a second and then found ground. Dan's stomach twisted the fermenting beer into a watery knot. He could envision the dogs' guts flying everywhere. But the squealing was no more.

He cut the wheel back, so he wouldn't bump again and rolled back. He cut the lights on "parking only," hopped out, running to the side of the fence. He peered through the tiny slats in the privacy fence. No lights at the Ruckers' house. Good. Dan the Man was sweating and sporting a newly acquired limp when he made it to the front of the Jimmy.

There lay Charlie, motionless, and bathed in a ghostly orange glow from the parking lights.

Dan could then see what part of the dog he had slid the tire on. The left side of Charlie's face was peeled back, the loose folds collectively hanging over the ear area, which was itself shifted slightly askew. The eye socket and eye was still there, just red and bloody with a white pus-like film spreading across the socket. The teeth now in a permanent show of aggression, with no cheeks to hide the massive incisors.

Dan the man turned away from the ghastly spectacle and threw up three of his fourteen beers. He was sick, panic-stricken, and suddenly very paranoid about being caught. With the injured leg, self-defense would have made sense. But this was a bit beyond self-defense. This wasn't a spur of the moment, lose your freakin' mind event. He had planned it. Planned it on the fly in a drunken rage, but planned it just the same. Camped out and waited like he was on a backyard hunting trip. This would not go well with a judge.

It only took Dan seven minutes to place Charlie inside a garbage bag, shore the dead weight into the back of the Jimmy, re-park the SUV outside the gate, remove the Saran wrap from the seat, and get in the shower.

Dan watched his leg bubble as he emptied the entire bottle of Hydrogen Peroxide onto it. Puncture wounds seemed to hurt worse than any slice he had ever taken. Out of the shower, he wrapped the wound tight with Neosporin caked between the wrap and his leg. He took five 200mg Ibuprofens and one muscle relaxer. He lay back on the bed, watched the ceiling fan rotate with a surreal calmness, and was asleep inside of three minutes.

2

No alarm clock was needed. The pulsating dullness underneath his bandage was a lot worse than he remembered it being last night. Getting out of bed was difficult. He would have to see a doctor later, but right now there were more pressing matters.

After dressing, he chugged some Pepsi and went to the side door. No crowd of onlookers gathered around the back of his Jimmy.

Murder makes you paranoid, don't it, Danny boy?

He pushed the thought out of his head.

Four more pain pills, but no muscle relaxers. He was driving today. Over the course of the next hour, Dan removed tufts of hair from his grill, the tire, the yard, and used a pair of pliers to bend the clasp on the run to the open position. That should wrap things up, almost. It was 9:24 A.M.

Dan grabbed his keys and cell phone and shut the house door. In under an hour, Charlie's leg-gnawing ass would be in Chamberlain Creek where the wildlife would finish him off in a week or so. He felt like a Goodfella. *You wronged da familia, youse gotta pay, Charlie. We gotta take a little ride, see?* He smiled as he rounded the back of the SUV. His smiled faded as he glanced in the back window.

Looking in, he saw the black plastic bag half chewed on one side. He moved his head this way and that, then cupped his hands on the window to make sure of what he was seeing. His eyes followed the crinkled curves and sharp folds of the shiny plastic as it disappeared into the hard-to-see space right up against the spot where the back seat met the packing space.

He tapped the window. Nothing. He felt strained, weirdly cautious, and a little like an idiot. What did he expect? This was crazy. He had smushed the dog under the chassis and again with the tire, on the head. No telling

how many bones he had splintered. And the tire on the head? No way
Charlie was alive. But then why was he feeling so shaky? And why was
the plastic so chewed looking on one side?

Maybe the damn thing did live at first. Maybe it came to and chewed at
nothing in particular in a wild zombie-like fashion with its half-working
mind until it bled out and died.

*But what if he's not dead? What if this mutt's mind is still twitching
around on autopilot? You gonna drive down the road with a Night of the
Living Dead canine in the back of the truck?*

That was a freaky thought. He didn't like to admit it, but he had been
afraid of Charlie. What about a half-dead, twitchy Charlie?

He would have to check.

He began covering that creeping fear with anger. Charlie would haunt
and taunt him no more. He was in control now. He opened the door, and as
it swung upward, Dan was hit by the foulest stench he had ever smelled. It
came boiling out of the back like a tidal wave born of a sewage treatment
plant. His head turned to the side and held his breath. Yes, Charlie was a
goner for sure. He backed up for a second to let the smell finish pouring
out. He would have to get a full sixty-dollar job, inside and out, from the
guys down on Noble Street.

He stared at the crumpled bag for a moment and then gave a quick look
to the neighbors' yards. No one out yet on this muggy, hot July morning.
He looked back at the carpeted space and realized for the second time just
how big Charlie was. He was taking the two thirty-nine gallon bags to their
length limit. He could see a nail from the paw pushed through the bag to
the right, stuck out and resting on the right sidewall of the truck. The tip of
Charlie's nose was barely visible through the chewed (*yeah, Danny, it's
been chewed on*) bag that rested near the upper-left corner of the back. The
first time he realized how large Charlie was, he was attempting to pick him
up and put him in the back of the Jimmy. He had been pumped with
adrenaline, but it had still been a bitch.

Lying on the right side of the trunk, next to the seat, was a very comfortable cap. No sports team or John Deere on the front, just a plain blue cap that he didn't want infected with dead-Charlie cooties. Without letting the creeps or smell have time to get to him, he quickly leaned forward, reached over the bag, and as his hand touched the cap, he heard the plastic under his chin rustle.

He flew backwards, narrowly avoiding the gnashing teeth as they came for his jugular. The back of Dan's head slammed into the top of the Jimmy and kept going, along with Dan's body, as it hit the rock hard concrete behind him. His right leg immediately began to throb again. A new pain shot through the back of his head and lower back. His hand came up to his head as he lifted it off the driveway. He felt a drip. He had opened his hand back up trying to catch himself. He looked up at the truck and saw a motionless black bag.

"Jeeeez! You alright Danny?"

It was Phil Rucker. He had a paper in his hand and was slowly and curiously approaching Dan from the middle of his yard. Dan moved to get to his feet, just not as quickly as he had intended to.

"Damn bee! I'm allergic!" Dan lied. No reason to throw in the allergy, but if you're going to lie, why not lie well?

"Ahhh."

Seemed to be enough of an explanation for a Saturday morning.

A nod of the heads, smiles exchanged, and it was over. The staleness of a thousand and one rotten sausages penetrated his nostrils again. He had a rotting animal in his truck whose brain was still functioning. No. That made no sense. If the dog was rotting, then it had to be dead already. Maybe he was imagining things.

Overbearing murderous guilt maybe?

No. His conscience was not nagging that badly, was it? The bandage on his hand was beginning to pull on the wound. The wrap on the thigh was not so bad, caked with Neosporin. Dan moved forward with head turned, but eyes forward. He looked at the bag again. It was in the same position. He listened like a deer in the woods for the sound of labored breathing. Nothing.

He was tiring himself out early. His head was throbbing, his lower back ached like an old man's, his hand would have to be wrapped again, and the dressing on his leg was red in spots. It was leaking. He placed his hands on his hips and realized he was breathing heavily. Looking down, he realized something else.

"Wonderful, you idiot."

He smiled in spite of himself. His 14k link chain hung down across his slightly hairy chest. It had fallen out of his shirt when he leaned over and hit the bag. He laughed again. "You got me, Charlie. I'll give you that. You got me one last time, bitch." Dan smiled a surly smile at the bag. "Too bad I'm at the top of the food chain, huh, Charles?"

That made the pain in the back of his head feel a little better. He leaned forward with a little more confidence this time. He shook his head back and forth in a too-bad-for-ya' motion.

"Sorry, Charlie."

He laughed again and slammed the trunk back down. The next twenty minutes he spent in the house doctoring his wounds while the air conditioner in the Jimmy forced some of the smell out the open windows. His leg was horrible. That would be another doctor bill and stitches. More money.

He was shocked to find himself growing woozy at one point. He had to stop and look away for a minute before rebandaging the wound. He cursed the dead mutt in the car the whole time. Dan walked to the backyard and sprayed the screen door and decking with degreaser and let the hose go. He finally had to scrub to get some of the blood off the deck. He turned the hose on the spot in the yard that had stained the grass with blood. Covering your tracks was hard work. He was sweating again as the southern humidity worked its magic.

One last thing before he left. He didn't want Karen showing up to find Charlie missing and start asking questions of the neighbors or poking around. She wouldn't take his call anyway, so he would leave a quick message and be on his way. He took out his cell and dialed her number.

"- leave a message at the beep."

"Hey, it's me. Look, I don't how to say this, but, umm, Charlie was hit, got off his chain, anyway, didn't make it. I'll uh, take care of it, you know. Anyway, just call if you uh- "

Beeeep!

"Hello? What? What did you say? What happened? What's wrong with Charlie?"

Karen sounded frantic and angry. He needed to calm her down or she would be over here asking a bunch of damn questions.

"It's okay. Hold on – I said he was hit… early this morning I guess. I'm going to bury him myself. Look – "

Click.

"HEY!" Dan looked at the phone like it was an alien weapon. Another first for the not-so-lady of the house. She had never, in all their time of dating and holy matrimony, hung up on Dan the Man.

"Crazy bitch."

He hung the phone up. The Vaseline and Neosporin felt mushy-weird on his leg, but that was okay because it was keeping the bandage from grabbing at the crusty and still partially open wound. He looked at his hand again. Nasty. No Palmolive commercials for me.

Dump the mutt, go to the emergency room, wait, no... Doctor Philstein was open 'til twelve on Saturday and that would cost less, and then come home and get drunk again. A Dan the Man Plan. And this time, he would call the Shitsters. That was what Karen called Mark and Jason. She thought they were a little on the loud and brash side, especially in restaurants, and maybe they were. Who gives a shit? Maybe I'll call all the guys from the pool hall, Billy and Weezel from the garage. Hell, maybe I'll call every damn person I know after I get this fleabag in the water, and we'll just wreck the damn house. How about that little *miss clickadeeclickclick?*

He winced as he raised his leg to get in the truck. The white bandage was speckled with a marble-like maroon, like a Mummy with chicken pox. The truck was cool and most of the smell had dissipated. Yes, there was still a meaty, graveyard stench that would remain for some time.

He clicked the seat-belt and repositioned the rearview mirror to reflect slightly down to the back of the truck. That crackling of the muddy plastic – *I know it was my chain; I'm sure of it* – was still pushing up the goose pimples on his arm. If the dog had been alive, then it probably shit itself. That's what stinks. That and the blood. No matter. If he wasn't dead now, he would be dead after the toss into the creek.

He cut out of the driveway and slammed on his brakes. A red Celica swerved and cut him off right in the middle of the road. It was Carol at the wheel, and Karen was already out of her door before the car had come to a stop. The expression on her face was sadness mixed with rage.

"Where's Charlie?" Karen shouted. Carol just stood behind her open door and watched like a hawk.

"Whoa, calm the hell down. We almost had a head on."

Karen's face was stern. Unwavering. It did not change. Her eyes piercing his skull.

"I said, *where's Charlie?*"

He wanted to get her inside so he could talk, but he thought of Charlie in the back, possibly still moving or breathing. Then there was the gnawed plastic, and he had already said the animal was dead. He held his right hand to his side so she couldn't see it. He had pulled his shorts down to cover the spotty bandage, and if Karen were to lift up the back of his shirt, she would see half of his underwear and ass hanging out.

"Look, I'm taking care of it. Calm, down." He could see her brow crunch down harder and harder each time he told her to calm down. "I know you must be upset, and we'll talk about it when I get back. We need to talk anyway," he murmured, looking over at Carol's skeptical face, "and set things right so – "

"Set things right," Karen was looking at Dan like he had just wet himself in public. Then she did something that crawled all over Dan and his little ego. She looked at Carol and gave an incredulous and confidential laugh. To Carol she said, "Like it's a broken bone or some shit'?"

Dan was on trial and his Defense Attorney wasn't doing his job. Then she started screaming at the top of her lungs.

"WHERE – "

"Will you – "

"IS – "

"just listen – "

"CHARLIE!"

"for a sec – "

"WHERE?"

Now she was a banshee in the middle of the street, screaming so all the neighbors could be a part of their business. Carol had that *you go girl* look on her face. Her bitch friend was somehow nagging it along silently behind her. Then he saw Karen's face change to confusion. She put her hand up to her nose and mouth, and it hit him about the same time. The smell.

She ran to the back of the truck, slung the door open, and turned her head away. She immediately began crying.

"Oh, my God."

"Listen," he stopped short, searching for words and explanations that were not there. Karen stared, drilling a hole through his head with hate-ray vision. He was transparent.

"Where was he hit?"

She was turning in panicky circles, looking for some sort of clues on the asphalt. Dan stuttered slightly, looked over at the black bag, still worrying about movement. And what if she sees the chewed part of the bag? What then? He was a cop killer sitting in the middle of an FOP party.

"He got off his run, Karen. Can we just – "

She was running up the driveway

"Karen!"

A black car beeped, then slowly went around. A white head of hair and a frown. He was on display again. He wanted to leave, but couldn't. The investigation was still under way. Court was still in session. Karen opened the fence and disappeared behind it.

Should have left it open. That's all right, I would have closed it afterward. Get the story straight.

Carol's smug face eyed him as he closed the back of the truck, his eyes still on the gate. She would see the flattened grass from the wheels, or maybe a stray tuft of hair he had missed, or blood. He was busted twice over. He would be on that animal cop TV thing. Dog Killer brought to justice.

A few awkward moments later, Karen came out of the gate flying, tears streaming down her face. Clear streaks of rage and confusion. He wasn't sure what that meant, if anything. What was the verdict?

"I want him buried at the cabin, near the edge of the woods, away from the drive on the right side."

Another change in Dan the Man's plan. What could he say?

"Fine."

She and Carol were in the car before he could add anything else, not that he had anything else left to say. The investigation was over, at least. He was acquitted. Lack of evidence.

Buried at the cabin. Wonderful. A forty-five minute drive and, with the hole digging, a good three hour thorn in the side for Dan.

When he arrived at Lowe's, Dan parked in the huge empty space near the main road and left the car running. The smell was becoming unbearable. A pick, some gloves, and a shovel (he thought they had one at the cabin, but if they didn't, that would be a hell of a drive to get one). Another quick stop at the Shell. A half-case of Bud. He hit I-20 as the sun reached its apex, veiled by a dull haze of cloud cover. It was beginning to rain and the oversized drops thumped away at his windshield. The Stones belched out "Anastasia, screamed in vain" on the radio. The windows were cracked, and that helped a little with the smell. He could handle a few raindrops on his arm.

Karen's investigation with her accomplice Carol was still fresh in his head. The rain trampled his windshield, millions of tiny warriors, the wipers fighting them off valiantly. Ten minutes into the drive he was so absorbed in Karen's anger and that awful, penetrating and accusing look she had thrown at him, he only looked in the rearview mirror five times a minute instead of twenty. The gnawed plastic still crinkling in his mind.

Who did she think she was to just accuse him of something, scream at him in front of everybody and their brother, and then demand that he bury the dog at her parent's cabin? He had a good mind to pop the rear up and let the next big bump carry the mutt bouncing onto the center line. No. Karen would eventually come to her female senses and come home.

Fifteen minutes into the drive, wipers slapping the sides of the windshield, he saw the first one. A Heinz 57, as his dad used to say. A mutt. The mixed breed was sitting on its haunches in the median. Sheets of rain moved through the tall grass causing it to undulate like a sea during a Northeaster. The dog was sitting there between the two split sections of I-20 in the downpour. It was a wet-dog statue. When the truck passed by, Dan looked over at the odd sight.

"There's one of your buddies that doesn't know when to get out of the rain."

Dan's eyes were about to check the back of the Jimmy again when he saw the mutt follow the truck with a turn of its head. It was almost as if it was –

No. That's ridiculous.

For a split second, Dan could have sworn the mutt was actually looking, not at the truck, but at him. He checked the side mirror. As much as he could tell from a tiny mirror in a rainstorm, the dog was still turned in his direction, staring.

Staring? That was crazy. He laughed it off without conviction. He looked again in the rearview mirror.

Nothing.

3

Officer Ben Braswell was working the Heflin Fork Junction. It was lunchtime, which didn't mean too awful much for the town of Heflin. A little more traffic, but nothing to write home about, and for a township of around 4,700, that was to be expected.

"You there, Ben?"

Ben responded, "Yeah, Sally. Whatcha got?"

"Weeeelllllll," she sounded amused in a way, "I figured you might be the one for this. There's an old fellow named Jeremiah Wills who's waiting for you over at the Pet Cemetery. I know you don't like spoilers, so I'll just say it's not the usual run of the mill high school kids with nothing to do on Friday night kind of thing. This one's a doozy."

He looked up as an oversized SUV soared through the intersection. The numbers on his dashboard flashed 56. Not only were they going 16 miles an hour over the speed limit, and not only were they in a huge, gas-guzzling piece of ego, they were also on the phone. That was grounds for a good pistol whipping. But there was a mystery brewing; he could feel it.

"What about a little teaser, Sal?"

It was a few seconds before she responded. "Well, I know you like the King stuff, so here it is. You remember that movie where they kept burying people in the cemetery to bring 'em back?"

"Yeah. *Pet Sematary*."

"Better than that."

Ben smiled. He felt like a little boy. Most things in the police line of work were the same, over and over again. Domestic disputes, drunk drivers, tickets, warrants, fights on the weekend, and more drunks. But every now and then, something reared its head that led to a little bit of a Matlock mystery. He had thought about detective and had a prior opportunity. He loved the mystery of it, but had turned it down. He knew that behind most mysteries there was nothing more than someone with an unworthy reason to hurt, kill, or frighten someone. It was the real thing: the little kids that were hurt, or the pregnant mom knifed and dead in her trailer – of which he wanted no part. That was the real of it. That was life. Locking horns with monsters like that and letting that stuff follow you home at night was not the path for him.

At the ripe age of 42, what had peaked his interest in sci-fi, horror films and creepy books happened over two years ago in his home town of Ridley. But nothing had come around like that since. Now, Sally was hinting at something big. A real big something. And knowing how much he liked King, saying it was bigger than *Pet Sematary*, well, that meant something. Sally wasn't going to yank his string for nothing.

He forgot the SUV and the cell phone, put the cruiser in drive, and headed west.

*****

The mutt's name, the one still sitting in the median like a statue in a hurricane, was Chancellor. He had gotten loose, himself, unlike Charlie, and had forged along I-20 for an adventurous hour and a half before an eighteen-wheeler had clipped his backend at seventy-five miles per hour. Chancellor sat in the wavy grass with a spinal column that had snapped in five places and a left hind quarter that was hanging on by an inch-wide piece of stretched skin. He felt no pain.

He knew he could not make the trip, but was drawn anyway. It was as if his old master had called him, but this was a much stronger voice.

Chancellor dropped down in the tall grass so others in the big, colorful machines wouldn't see him and began to drag himself through the slopping wet grass west on I-20. He was obeying a new master. This master he could not see, but just the same, could feel all throughout his broken flesh.

Dan took the off ramp, hung a right, and then hung a quick left right past the Huddle House. This was County Road 204, or Leatherwood if you lived nearby. It was the first of many backroads. Several turns and a couple of old iron bridges were all that stood between Dan and his 12-pack of beer.

Crossing the first bridge, he noticed the creeks were mud-brown and that the rain was churning them to brackish rapids. That had been plan one. Different creek, though. It would have been quick and painless and over with in five seconds. Now he had to dig, dig, dig. His leg was starting to throb, and the cold half-case was looking mighty tempting. He would be there shortly anyway, and he had never seen a cop out this way in all the times he and Karen had come here. Of course, a DUI would not be the way to end the day.

Small holes that tarnished the warped back roads were now miniature ponds of unknown depth. He swerved to miss them. He glanced in the rearview again and then reached for the case, ripping open the handle on top and feeling the friendly cold of aluminum inside his hand. As Dan topped the next rise, he saw the police lights. Dan quickly shoved the beer back down into the case and slowed to a snail's pace.

It was sprinkling now and two cops were standing and talking next to their car just off the road. It didn't look like a road block, so Dan raised a friendly hand. The officer facing him raised a hand back, and the officer with his back to him turned to look. Dan kept on trucking. He glanced over at the worn cemetery sign. The only pet cemetery within a hundred miles, as far as he knew. Some kids must have stolen Sparky's headstone or left their beer bottles around a campfire. He watched the lights disappear in his rearview and decided to take a little shortcut.

A mile down the road there was a dirt road that cut to the right. After four miles of deep ruts and a couple of steep grades, Dan would come to the cabin from the south side instead of the mostly paved north route. It

was an extra couple of miles but no cruiser was about to brave these roads.
Dan could go ahead and start on the first of many beers.

After taking the road, he grabbed the beer back out and chugged the
first one. A loud burp echoed satisfaction as the Jimmy bumped and
ground along, wheels slipping sideways on the wet clay, then finding
traction on a few rocks jutting out. He was moving slowly forward.

Beer number two. Now things were rolling. Charlie flopped around in
the back, forgotten save the smell. Dan maneuvered down a steep grade
and then the road evened out a little, though it narrowed considerably. He
puttered along for another half mile and threw the next empty can out the
window and into the woods.

"Time for number three, Charlie!" he said with a smile and looked into
the rearview. As he came over the next rise, Dan hit his brakes and slid for
a few feet before stopping just short of a head-on with a police car. His
hand that was hovering over the case of brew retreated quickly.

*****

"Officer Ben Braswell."

He greeted the old man. He was old indeed. Looked to be in his early
seventies with dark chocolate skin and ghost white hair. His plain brown
shirt and work pants were soaked, and he didn't seem to mind.

Instead of waiting in his truck and staying out of the rain, he had
chosen to wander around and look for clues while waiting on the police.
Jeremiah was paid a minimal sum to come out Saturday and Sunday
morning and clean up any messes left the night before. The owners didn't
want some old lady coming out to see their dearly departed and find
pooch's grave littered with bottles of cheap wine and beer.

"Nice to meet you, sir."

"The same. So what do we got?"

The old man made a face that said "*Whew, wait till you see this.*" He started walking through the front of the graveyard, and Ben followed.

"Well, I came a little late this morning. Grabbed my five gallon bucket and – "

Ben lost the rest of the old man's sentence as he approached the first tree line. There were lumps of wet Earth here and there. As he scanned the open spots to where the road cut the graveyard in half, he saw lumps of turned mush everywhere.

"-so I immediately called you guys. This . . . this just ain't the normal, well, it ain't normal period."

Ben couldn't stop staring around himself, turning in circles like a dog about to lie down. There must have been over fifty lumps on this side of the road alone.

As if reading his mind, Jeremiah said, "Other side's the same, sir."

"My lord."   His astonishment was real. This would have taken a massive amount of work and more than one person to hit them all in one night.

"Do you know how deep they were buried?"

"I think, from the one or two I've actually seen buried, about three feet, maybe four at the most. Think the law says three, maybe. Course I doubt it's enforced, ya know."

Ben looked at the dirt road leading to the back of the cemetery.

"Did you drive down in here at all?"

"No sir. And I looked myself. No tracks that I could tell. No new beer bottles either, I guess cause it rained a little last night, ya know."

Yes, this was a good one. A creepy one for sure.

"I wonder how many they got?" He was talking to himself, but the old man answered.

"One hundred and eleven," he spoke slowly and accentuated the number with purpose and finality.

Ben was amazed again. He said, "You counted them all?"

"Yes, sir." This was spoken as if Jeremiah had no idea why this was so curious a feat.

Ben shook his head. No tracks, over a hundred graves tilled up, all in one night.

Ben asked, "Is there a back way in?"

"Well, that's where it gets interesting."

With that, Jeremiah began walking toward the back of the graveyard on a diagonal path to the road that cut the tree line in two. As Ben followed he looked at one of the graves as he passed. Macy – A loving companion for 15 years – 2001. The headstone was marble, and he wondered how much it cost. Two or three hundred? Maybe more?

By the grassy build-up of one grave, he noticed a spot of dirt that rose from a puddle. The low-lying land must flood often. He wondered if they had trouble with any boxes floating to the surface if it really came down. Then he glanced at what looked like a paw print in the muddy spot. Tiny. Maybe a raccoon.

After dodging a lot of headstones and walking for a moment on the road that led to the back of the graveyard, Ben saw himself that indeed, the only tracks on the dirt road seemed to be the ones they were making.

"I just can't believe they got so many, ya know?"

Jeremiah stopped in the road, the back part of the graveyard now surrounding them, oaks and maples spreading their gnarled arms out to protect the graves from the drizzle. Back here it looked the same as the front. There was something about the graves that bothered Ben, but he couldn't put his finger on it yet.

Jeremiah pointed to the forest behind the last of the cemetery.

"Behind the trees there, about a hundred yards, is a road that runs all up and down the mountains between here and Lake Cleburne. Some motorbikes you can hear back there in the summer, tearin' it up. They coulda come in that way. But the interesting thing, sir, is the *ones* they took."

Officer Braswell looked up from trying to pierce the tree line with his gaze.

"Excuse me?"

"The ones they took. Not too many people would've noticed maybe, but I been workin' this yard for about twelve years. I double checked myself on this one, and that's part of the reason I actually counted the graves. You see, they only took the dogs."

Jeremiah let that one set for a minute, and so did Ben. Ben mumbled a question to himself and Jeremiah both, just under their breath. "No cats, snakes, or hamsters, or – lizards? None?" Jeremiah shook his head in the negative.

That was weirder than it sounded on the surface, and the old man had picked up on it too. How would the kids, or whoever it was, know exactly which ones were the dogs? And out of over a hundred, never digging up a cat? How could that possibly be a coincidence? Yes, this was a doozy all right.

Jeremiah said, "That's the interesting thing. Now here's the creepy thing. And this you'll have to see on your own. I've already been over there, and I might think it's a prank, but just the same, I ain't goin' *back* over there." Jeremiah pointed to the back corner of the graveyard.

Ben stared for a moment at the old man. He was serious, hand still out and finger extended. He wasn't moving.

"O-K . . . "

Ben started over towards the back left corner, where the cemetery ended and the tree lines converged after a short space of no more than five or so yards. As he approached it, he saw nothing out of the ordinary. There were a few dug-up graves here and there, just like everywhere else. There were patches of grass and smaller patches of mud, slickened orange spots pooled with water. His shoes sinking down into the soggy sponges of grass, carefully avoiding the mud.

He was on top of it when he finally saw it. He could only look in disbelief as the rain trickled off his hat and poured in front of his face. In the patch of mud that spanned no more than four feet of waterlogged ground, there were tufts of hair and a few bones, some with pieces of gray-looking flesh still clinging madly to them. They lay in the middle of what looked like a wagon trail from the old west. Every single one of the animals must have been dragged through this one muddy spot and into the woods beyond. Ben stared into the woods and could see nothing. He wanted to go in further, but like old Jeremiah, something deep down told him that egos only got you so far in life.

He walked with the old man back to his car and called Lacky and Wheels to the scene. After asking about a way around to the back of the cemetery, he thanked Jeremiah for his help and waited for his buddies. They only took five minutes to come down from their spot at the entrance. Word had got around through Sally that something weird was going on at the graveyard. They wanted to see for themselves.

As Ben drove off, he finally put his finger on the strange feeling he had about the graves. And though the old man hadn't mentioned it, he was sure he had caught on to that too. He had thought there was something odd about the way the graves had been dug up. The thing was, it didn't look like there was any digging at all. At least not with a shovel from above.

4

Dan stared in disbelief at the police cruiser in front of him. There was absolutely no way this cop car could have made the trek he just did. The foot-deep ruts, not a quarter mile in, the lake of water that spanned the road's width and ran for fifteen feet, a tar pit of quicksand for sure, and then the forty-five degree incline down the mountain he had just descended. These would disembowel a car in a heartbeat. And what was a cop doing out in the middle of the woods at 1:30 in the afternoon?

The cop swung his door open. Dan looked around for a breath mint, gum, crackers, motor oil, anything to erase the smell of beer from his breath. He had only had two beers and certainly wasn't going to blow over the limit, but that didn't mean anything, not really. What mattered now was that his breath smelled like beer, he had almost grilled a cop car, and there was a dead animal in the back.

There was something else that bothered Dan as he watched the policeman walk around to his side of the car, turning sideways to squeeze between the cars. The cop was moving . . . slowly . . . cautiously. The cop's reserved approach made Dan nervous, more nervous than the regular amount of nervous you get when a cop pulls you over.

Dan rolled his window down and let the sprinkling rain trickle its way into the truck. The cop was a middle-aged fellow and nice looking enough, but there was something going on in the cop's mind as he scoured the inside of Dan's truck. The rain didn't seem to bother the man as he looked down at Dan. When he saw the beer, he leaned over sideways to get a better look. He knew the cop could see the broken top of the case sticking up.

"How many, son?"

"I had two, sir, after I pulled off the road back there – I mean, I know that doesn't make it alright . . . I was just heading up to the cabin."

Dan had reflexively pulled out his wallet with his driver license. The cop wasn't asking for it. Another unnerving brick that was piling on top of Dan's wall of paranoia.

"Do you always co- "

The officer stopped short and leaned back away from the car.

"What exactly is that smell, son?"

"My dog, sir. Got hit this morning. I'm taking him to the cabin to bury him. Know I shouldn't be drinking while I'm behind the wheel, but he was just, you know, a good friend." He was laying it on thick and felt stupid for saying the dog was his buddy. But hey, it fit, didn't it? Maybe this was one of those animal lovers or something.

The look on the officer's face changed again, and in a strange way that didn't quite jibe with the answer he had given. Dan could feel himself teetering on the edge of an invisible cliff. He had said *something* that the cop didn't care for, and it made him more than just uncomfortable, it made him nervous as shit.

The cop stood erect and headed for the back of the truck, head still turned slightly to keep an eye on Dan. Dan began thinking about the chewed plastic bag. That was a clue that Karen might have overlooked, but a cop would catch it quick. Then the policeman did something that Dan had to actually convince himself he was seeing. In the rearview, Dan watched as the cop lowered his hand ever so slightly to his right side and unsnapped his holster.

Dan went from seeing himself in a green, concrete room for the night, to seeing his wide-open and unblinking eyes collecting rainwater in the middle of the forest. A voice bellowed from the rear.

"Sir?"

He could see half of the officer in the mirror now, the other half hid by the mirror.

"Could you step out slowly and come to the rear of the vehicle?"

Step out slowly *? What the hell is going on?*

Maybe it was Karen. Did her dad know the police in this area? *Sure officer, just make it look like an accident, and then bury the sonofabitch with the dog. Then meet us girls at the cabin, and we'll all give you a hummer for your troubles.* Dan's mind was thumping with paranoia.

He opened his door, slowly, nervously, and walked to the rear of the vehicle, wallet and license still in hand. The cop now wore a frown and eyed Dan cautiously. He took the license and looked back and forth, from license to Dan, from Dan to license.

"You mind opening the back?"

It wasn't a question.

Dan stole a glance at the cop's hip. His holster was unsnapped. Dan moved like he was holding dynamite and raised the back.

"Any weapons in the vehicle or on your person?"

"No, sir."

It was a lie. It came out before he could help himself. There was a nine in the glove compartment.

The dead-flesh rot seeping out the back of the Jimmy seemed to be affecting Dan more than the cop. Dan watched the unclipped holster from the corner of his eye. He could suddenly see himself being thrown into the back with the stinking dog, a big wolf grin on the cop's face as he closed them up.

"Your dog?"

As if he had stolen someone else's dead dog?

Assuringly, "Yes, sir. Mine and my wife's, sir."

Garbage-can Chirizo. What was this cop looking for? The silence that followed, along with the cop's poker face, racked Dan's nerves. Filling the silence was necessary.

"Just taking him up to the cabin, 1114 LaTrace." He pointed like a schoolkid. "Burying him next to the cabin."

He had done nothing wrong, at least nothing this cop should know about. But cops always make you sweat. They know you've done *something* wrong.

"Gotta tag on him?" The cop nodded at the bag.

Not a question, a command.

The last thing Dan wanted to do was get close to the dog, and now the cop was motioning to the torn bag around the head area. The investigation was somehow being reopened by a local pig-hick. Dan just wanted to end this.

Staring at the bag, he could see another slight tear (*chewed through, Danny boy*) in the bag just above the front leg quarter. Dan leaned over the back and slowly reached for the chewed portion of the bag, keenly aware that he could not see what the cop was doing behind him. The teeth were next to his hand and a strange cop was standing behind him in the woods, deep enough in the forest so that no one would hear his screams. If the cop had noticed the chewed look to the corner of the bag, he hadn't shown it.

Dan would fix that right now. He grabbed the edge of the tear, keeping his hand as far away from what was inside as possible, and tore it open even wider, revealing a tiny piece of aluminum, dyed red. The collar was still attached, but the skin had been ripped and shoved in crumpled folds underneath the collar. The head and teeth were slightly hidden by the upper part of the bag, and a good thing too, because the skin that was folded up on itself all around the collar had come from somewhere.

"Dog's name?"

The cop wanted to see if he knew before he looked. What did this guy think? That he was scraping dogs off the highway for personal use? This was creepy.

"Charlie, sir?"

Another nod. Great. Now for a slimy, meaty game of Operation. Don't touch the sides Dan or – EEEENNHHHHH ! A flash of a famous painting flashed in Dan's mind. It was a Bosch. There were body parts thrown in a large frying pan and a little fellow of questionable merit was having a good old smorgasbord of arms and legs. Welcome to Hell, enjoy the smell. His hand slid next to the soggy pelt. Dan grimaced. He moved to the side a little so the cop could see the tag in the palm of his hand.

The cop leaned over to see. He seemed to approve silently, but looked a little confused. Correct name. Good thing Karen had gotten the prissy little nametag after all.

"Closer please, son."

It was like the policeman just couldn't believe his own eyes. Dan obliged and pulled it out a little. In doing so, you couldn't hear it, but Dan could feel something giving a little. Maybe a tendon or muscle, or maybe a bone cracking loose somewhere deep in Charlie's chest. His stomach went weak.

"Thank you."

Dan let go and Charlie went limp back into his resting spot. There was something about that bothering Dan, but again, something he couldn't quite put his finger on.

"That pick and shovel brand new?"

The cop motioned, again with his head only, keeping his hands to his side, at the tools laid up with their handles on the back seat.

"Yes, sir. Got the receipt if you need it?" He did.

This was asinine. He almost reached into his right pocket after the receipt with the hand that had just rubbed all over Dead Charlie. He hesitated momentarily, then realized that he couldn't use his bandaged left hand if he had wanted to. There was nowhere to wipe his hands but on his nice Khaki shorts. He tried not to let his disgust show as he slid his slightly wet hand into his pocket and pulled out the receipt. At least he wouldn't stain the outside where people could see.

"Lowes . . . twenty-seven fourteen. Alrightee, Mr. Strawburg. Sorry for the trouble."

The cop seem to relax a little, but still had his thinking cap on, like he was trying to multiply double digit numbers in his head. But he was walking away now, and that was all that mattered. He screwed up his name and that was fine. Dan wasn't about to correct him. Double Jeopardy. Acquitted twice. Time to move on.

The cop stopped at the front of his cruiser. He spoke as if he was embarrassed to have forgotten about it.

"Lay off the brew 'til you reach the cabin, hear?"

"Yes, sir," as sincerely as he could manage.

"We uh... ," the cop spoke carefully, "had a little trouble at the Pine Crest Cemetery over the hill there." He pointed behind Dan. "Know anything about that."

Dan's confusion was authentic and the cop could see it.

"No, sir."

The cop moseyed back to his car as the rain sprinkled gently on Dan. Dan's feathers had been ruffled, but there were no silver bracelets on his wrists. That was a huge plus. He pulled the Jimmy back and moved to the side, as did the cop. Dan gave a "thank you" nod as he passed by the cop's window, then he watched the policeman disappear over the hill. How the cop was going to make it out, he didn't know and didn't care. If he got stuck, he could radio for help while Dan kicked back with his beer at the cabin.

*****

Ben shook his head. What were the odds of running into a guy a half-mile behind the cemetery with a dead dog in the back of his truck, and it not being the guy responsible for the disinterring? But the pick and shovel were brand new like the man said, and if he had done something with all those dogs, there would have been much more of a mess in the back of his little SUV. There was the bandage on his hand he kept trying to hide, and the one on his leg. That was a little strange. A little strange, but not a lot strange, and right now he was only following uber-strange. This noontime, backwoods drinker would have to take a back seat. He watched the wipers intermittently rub the droplets from his view as he looked for the turn at the foot of the hill the old man had told him to take.

*****

It took Dan nearly twenty minutes to make the next mile. He could see himself sliding off the wet clay into a ditch and being stuck, walking the rest of the way, or maybe hitting a car full of kids or a four-wheeler as he topped each little rise. Considering what had just happened, Dan was amazed at his own propensity to grab a beer and chug it. The cold aluminum was calling his name. But the paranoia seed had sprouted and was taking root in the conspiratorial section of his worrisome mind.

You did something you shouldn't of and now sweet Karma come 'round to kick that ass, baby boy.

Dan looked in the rearview mirror. He thought about how Charlie had it coming. He was the aggressive one. He was the one barking and growling at him in his own yard. He hadn't done anything wrong. Yes, Charlie had it coming.

Maybe so, Danny boy. But maybe, just maybe, you got it coming too.

Dan looked in the rearview mirror again. He jiggled in his seat as he bumped over the next rise. Dan felt a bad weight on his shoulders. Did Karen deserve this? He pushed the thought out of his head.

I don't deserve this. This is bullshit. Caught screwing one time and everything goes to shit. Pissed women, strange cops, mad old ladies, and smelly dead mutts in your vehicle. I'm the one who doesn't deserve this!

Dan followed the next sharp curve and saw what could be categorized as a shallow pond about twenty feet ahead. It ran for almost twenty feet. Although it couldn't be too awful deep, he wasn't taking any chances. He rolled up his window and gassed it. He parted the muddy water and it sprayed up into the air like a jet boat's rooster tail. The windshield was a smudgy brown for a second and then the wipers crossed it.

Dan saw a white fluff at the front corner of the truck and then he heard and felt a thud. He let off the gas and drifted quickly to a stop in the last four feet of the puddle. Without thinking, he leapt out and landed in four inches of sludge in his tennis shoes. He could feel the cool water rush in over his socks. Looking back, he saw something lying in the gently running water next to the puddle, off in a miniature drainage ditch and slightly covered with an inch or two of water. What he was seeing, he could not believe.

It was a dog. Another dog. It was some kind of big, black and white, fluffy mutt that must have weighed in at around forty-five pounds. He had actually run over a dog, after lying about Charlie all this time, and that was just, well, he didn't know what that was. A hell of a coincidence, he guessed.

He looked around for an owner, but nobody was around. And who would be way out here walking their dog in the rain? No one. He looked down at his shoes and realized he couldn't even see his shoes. Only ankles and a little bit of socks.

"Jesus!"

Dan could feel the ground under foot. At least it was solid and his truck wouldn't have to be pulled out of the mud by some money-grubbing wrecker service. But the $120 Nikes had suddenly depreciated about $115. He sloshed through the water and stopped as he approached the dog. Its ass was in the air, but its body was lying flat. And that coat wasn't pure white. It was muddy in parts and black in some spots. And those black splotches were familiar somehow. Different. As he tilted his head to get a look around the uptilted butt-end of the dog, he saw part of the head. It had the look of burnt charcoal and singed hair. The front end of his truck had not done that.

He was getting an uneasy feeling. That primeval warning switch, that hardwired caution beacon was flashing bright red. How did a dog that looked like it had caught fire end up in the middle of a muddy pool in the middle of nowhere? He could suddenly feel eyes on him from behind. Dan turned around and looked in the back of his truck, half expecting Charlie to be staring at him through the window.

Nothing.

He looked back at the black and white spectacle lying in the drain water. Now it was looking at him.

Dan froze.

Its head had tilted sideways and upward, its back still perpendicular to its hindquarter. The creepy canine yogi was as still as concrete, water dripping from its hairy jowls. Dan could see its singed, filmy eyes, and they were fixed on him. He was afraid to move. Worse still, that sense of something just *not being right* increased exponentially. Why was this dog not whimpering in pain? Its back was obviously broken. But it was silent, and the silence was deafening.

Then it smiled at him. It was showing its teeth in an aggressive gesture, surely. But Dan remembered those dogs from Funniest Home's Video where the dogs were taught to "smile," and that's all he could bring to mind.

Maybe it's smilin' at you, Danny boy. Maybe you just haven't got to the punchline yet.

Dan turned and ran, as fast as anyone can run in dirty, ankle-deep water, and jumped into his truck, muddy sneakers and all. He slammed the door and looked out the window. He was waiting for the animal to slam up against the window, teeth gnashing. But there was no fire and brimstone. No Cujo attacking the vehicle. He looked behind him in the side view mirror and saw the singed fluff moving.

Dan's eyes widened as the critter got to his feet, albeit awkwardly, and stood in the running water. It was staring at him in the side view. He suddenly felt something on his neck and swirled around.

Nothing.

He listened intently for breathing or movement of any kind. He was finished with questioning. His embarrassment and self-awareness disappeared on the spot. It was time to move. Get to the damn cabin and get inside and figure the rest out later. It was still light in the woods at 2:00, but light or no light, he didn't want to be out here anymore. Dan wanted to be near a telephone, refrigerator, and stove. He looked back at the side view.

Whitey was still there. Motionless.

Dan reached over and popped the glove box. He grabbed out the nine and took the safety off. Playtime was over. Stepping on the gas, he said a silent prayer, something he hadn't done in some time, that he would not get stuck in the mud. The Jimmy shot forward.

5

Ben almost drove right past the backend of the cemetery, even though he could have thrown a baseball and hit it from the road. It turns out that the undergrowth that secluded the trail where the dogs had disappeared on the other side, was just as thick and obtrusive on this side. A small white flash had caught his eye through the bushes (it ended up being an aluminum beer can). He got out and surveyed the surroundings. Nothing looked out of place, and on the way in he had not noticed any ruts in the road where it was mostly mud.

He pushed through the undergrowth as leaves released their water bombs onto his hat and shoulders. After forty yards of briars and bushes, he came out thirty yards shy of the back middle of the graveyard. He was off horizontally by about forty yards.

"Figures," he mumbled to himself with the reserve of someone who knows life is going to throw you curveballs every chance it gets.

He moved back through the brush to a point where he could almost see a narrow, doable path through the wet bushes that would parallel the graveyard and take him to the corner. As he made his way through the thicket, as he pushed large bushes to the side and got drenched in the process, he began replaying the conversation with the caretaker in his head. Three feet was the law. That's what the old man had said. That was about the depth of a meter stick. Ben started thinking about how long it would take him to dig up just one dog with a wet ground. Without his back giving out, he reckoned it would take about thirty minutes if he slung iron like a coal miner on crack. A hundred graves, divided by two to get the hours, and you were looking at 50 hours of digging like an insane robot. Add four drunk teenagers with a purpose and you get around 10 hours, nonstop, without anytime for beer. He carried the thought on as he carefully negotiated the exposed roots of a rather large oak.

Ben could see a possessed youth burying his pickaxe into the soft clay, muddied and wild-eyed. But after an hour of hard labor in the pouring rain, sobriety would find its way back and the thought of nine more hours wouldn't seem quite as cool as their initial game plan probably sounded. Besides, five drunken youths rarely made a concerted effort towards anything except buying more beer.

No, a hoax was looking more and more out of the question. He could hear Lackey's unusually sonorous laughter muffled by distance, trees, and rain. The two were probably about a hundred yards away at the entrance to the graveyard, cutting jokes and having a smoke instead of looking around like they should be. Just the same to them. Just passing time 'til the end of their shift on a rather slow day.

About fifteen minutes later, he peeked through a crowd of dripping branches and saw what had to be the corner stones in the graveyard. Ben was right on top of where the people would have to have drug the animals through. The ground was a little rocky here and scattered heavily with fallen branches, maybe blown down from last night's winds, and a couple of horizontal deadwoods that made leaving tracks impossible.

Scouring the shiny plant life on the forest floor, he noticed more tufts of hair. They had caught on some jagged rocks and one was hanging from a small piece of bark on a nearby pine. This gave him a direction.

He felt that hardwired switch flip itself instinctually again as he started forward on the trail, and slowed to a stop. What if there are five lunatic teens in the woods, rolling around with a bunch of dead dogs and stirring up some satanic rituals? But calling for Lackey and Wheels seemed unnecessary at this point and besides, he couldn't holler that far anyway. He certainly wasn't traipsing all the way back to the squad car to radio them. He would follow the trail for a moment and see what happened. The way it was looking, the trail would have to cross the road he came in on or turn and cut back across the tumble of road that led the short way out, the way he wasn't able to take on his way in. The fellow in the SUV could make it, but Ben would surely bottom out or snap an axle. So even if he needed these guys, it would take them forty minutes to drive around the way he had come. For now he would wait.

Ben found more and more as he paralleled the road he had turned onto. More pale skin, tufts of fur and another small bone or two. When there was no fur, there were bald spots on the ground from the mass exodus. He traveled a good two hundred or so yards when he was sure he had finally run out of a trail. Then he saw the drop off and walked over to it. Hanging on a small tree for safety, Ben leaned over the drop and saw water flowing down the small ditch to the side of the road. Below him was a clay hill speckled with rocks and a few baby pines. The eight-foot wide line of smoothed out clay that started from where he stood and ran down to the water's edge was unmistakable. There was a small pine that was bent over, imprinting into the wet clay like a living fossil. A mass of *something* had passed right over the edge.

The road below was extremely rocky and so the trail ended at the edge of the flowing water below. The woods across the way were impossible to see through with any clarity, but you could tell from the lay of the land that there was a decent-sized gully on the other side. He looked up and down the road, and from his vantage point could see no good spot to get down safely.

"Great."

On his trek back to the car he began turning this new information over in his head. Maybe the five drunken teenagers couldn't see what they were doing in the dark and . . . Yeah, right.

"Well, Ben," he said to himself, "you wanted uber-weird, you got uber-weird."

*****

As the Jimmy disappeared around the corner, Chuckles stood cockeyed with a perpendicular posture. The black skin stretched itself tight over her jowls. Not in giving with her name, Chuckles was not laughing. Her two front legs were fine, charred black and hairless in a stark contrast to the rest of her white, fluffy body, but structurally sound nonetheless. However, the back half of Chuckles formed a right angle to the rest of her body, making it so that her back right leg wasn't very far away from her front right leg. This made for a very awkward crab-hopping movement in order for Chuckles to move forward.

Chuckles had been a four-month resident at Pine Crest Cemetery ever since she had walked too close to her owner's backyard fire pit and fell fifteen feet to her end. She had yelped and hollered and scrambled blindly in the fire for a full thirty seconds before her screaming owner, eyes filled with tears already, had snagged her and pulled her smoking body from the burning brush and trash. He had used a 2x4x10 with a few nails on the end because that was all he could find in such a crazed rush. He cried over her for an hour and then put her in a trash bag so as not to dirty his pickup, which smelled of her burnt flesh all the way to the cemetery owner's house. Three hundred dollars and three days later she was in the ground with multitudes of other animals whose owners either loved their pets like kin, or simply knew what the alternative was and couldn't bear the thought.

Chuckles, a doggy version of Tommy Two Face, lurched forward with a gruesome little doggy hobble.

6

Karen was drawn up onto the edge of Carol's loveseat. She stared out the window and wondered why. Why did he do this? They had plenty of sex. Maybe it had tapered off a little lately, but three times a week was nothing to shake a stick at. Denise had told Carol last year that her and Tommy only had sex about once a month. That was after only six years of marriage. But Karen and Dan were still fresh, green newlyweds as far as most of their friends were concerned.

Carol sat a hot chocolate down on the small oak table next to her. She looked down and watched the tiny marshmallows bubble around for a moment. Nobody said a word. Carol wanted to tell her that she was better off without the sonofabitch, but she knew that, even considering what had happened, Karen still loved him. Hated him too, and with the same amount of passion, but loved him just the same. That's what made it hurt. Badmouthing wasn't the answer. She sat down softly next to her on the loveseat.

"I'm sorry, girl."

Karen offered a weak smile and nodded. It was all she could manage. During all of the madness and chaos, the one thing that had really made her feel happy and cry, both at the same time, was Charlie.

She had not wanted to go back to the house and be cornered by Dan, but she needed to feed Charlie. She had tacked a note to the door on day 2, and on day 3, Dan had called her cell and left another message. Along with his pitiful attempt at a half-hearted apology, he had mentioned that the dog had to be fed. He hadn't even tried to feed Charlie. How long had Charlie gone without food? Was it a ploy to get her to come over?

The next day, Karen had waited down the road from the house, a block over in the direction she knew he would *not* take to go to work, and then went to the house and fed Charlie herself. Yesterday, he had repeated his plea for her to feed the dog. He hadn't been outside to notice the dog food moved or that some of her things were already gone. Figured. What did she really expect?

She had smiled big for Charlie, gave him a couple of chicken legs before his main course, and explained to him that she would soon have a place and come back for him shortly. He had known something was wrong with his master. He whined and put his head across her elbows, something he rarely did. She began to sob uncontrollably.

"You okay, Girl?"

"I'll make it." There was a long pause as she looked out the window. She sighed deeply. It was drizzling outside, and the gray from the dark clouds dripped down onto everything, blurring the day.

"You know you can stay here as long as you need."

"Thanks."

Carol searched for something encouraging and found nothing. This was just the shits, plain and simple. Then she could see something change in Karen's face. She knew the look because she had seen it on Karen's face only once before. That was earlier today. It was the calm before the storm.

Karen turned her sad, angered, and mischievous face toward Carol. Carol's eyes widened in question.

With caution Carol asked, "What, girl?"

7

Ben was too busy running through impossible scenarios to be irritated with having to trek all the way back to his cruiser. All this just to pull back around to the road where the trail ended. As he made his way back to his cruiser, his foot landed on a clump of wet pine straw and he jilted sideways to keep balance. He managed to reach out and grab hold of a tiny sapling, saving himself from a fall. He was soaked, yes, but he didn't want to add insult to injury by having the back of his pants muddied.

There was always the road that the cruiser was parked on now; perpendicular to the road on which he had stopped the kid and the same road where the path disappeared. The old black fellow had said the road, where his cruiser was now parked, petered out at some stream after winding south for around three miles or so. He could take that and look for tracks, that is, if it didn't get too rough. Getting a tow truck to the middle of a rainy nowhere would be a bitch at 2:30 on Saturday, and would definitely not make Chief Nelson happy, and he respected Chief Nelson. It would actually make more sense to go back to the station and get the truck, but that would take too damn long and it would be almost 4:00 before he got back. That would only leave a few hours to look around. And this trail was just too fresh and too hot to call the dogs off now.

And a trail was exactly what Ben had found, right? It was a soggy nightmare trail of dead canines that someone was dragging through the woods to some unknown location. And for the first time, Ben got a shiver down the old spine. Why *would* they drag the dogs in *that* direction? It was much closer to park on the same road he had parked, only slightly further back, and then drag them in a straight line to whatever makeshift doggie hearse they were using. What would possess some wigged out people to drag the carcasses to the edge of the overhang and then toss them down?

Unless.

Unless they were throwing them into the back of a pickup or maybe . . . No, that didn't make sense either. That was still a good distance away and the extra dragging would have been way harder than just heaving them over the side of a truck. Of course, it was dark and raining, so maybe they got disoriented.

And how did they do it? Dig one up and then move it, or dig them all up and then pile them on something, like maybe a tarp, and then drag them all away? That was a thought that actually made sense. And the ground was wet, so digging would actually not be all that impossible. Still, the number was staggering. Then he thought about the jellybeans.

He, Marcy, and Jeff had been at the Southside Mall last year where they all took guesses on how many jelly beans had been packed into this over-sized, six- or seven-foot glass vase. An answer within 10 of the actual number would land you a brand new Toyota Avalon. No one won. And on top of that, they had all been over 2000 off the mark. He was sure there was someone with an algorithm that could peg it every time. Some java juiced nerd in some cubicle that would figure it out in less than a day. But there were surely none around the likes of Ridley and Lewiston.

So now he began to use the same useless algorithm he had used on the jellybeans. He took only medium-sized dogs and filled the bottom of a regular-sized pickup bed with them. Maybe twenty? Then multiplied by the thickness of a dog to account for, let's see, maybe three layers? That would be sixty or so dogs piled up in the back of a pickup without any passersby actually seeing anything. Especially at night when . . . but there were over a hundred and . . . but there could have been more than one truck and . . .

All dogs. All dogs and no cats. That was the kicker. That beat the time limits imposed by daylight. That beat the crazy amount of work necessary to dig that much dirt. That beat the lack of car or truck tracks so far. That beat it all. He had seen some of the grave markers. Some were brand spanking new. Others looked older than him and just as worn. There were even some wooden ones where you couldn't even make out a name. Not that it would help. Marcy's brother up in Philly had a 150 pound Newfoundland named Daisy. It was male. So how did they know?

As he reached his cruiser, he drove another mad scenario out of his head. The only one that made perfect sense, but then made no sense at all. He would wait a little before he strayed down that overgrown path. The road less traveled would have to wait. For now, running up on a group of underage, hung over Satanist seemed like a better alternative. Compared to the other scenario, it actually gave him a warm fuzzy feeling.

Ben did a forty-point turn so as not to slide in the trenches on each side of the soggy road. He drove back to the intersecting road and took a left. It was only fifty yards when he reached the point at which he had stopped before. Just to check, he drove another quarter mile. Sure enough, it was impassible with the cruiser. And just to think, if he had the truck, he could have reached the main road in no time. He turned around and drove slowly back to the spot where he had leaned over the hillside.

When he got out and walked over to the other side of the road, he knew he would not be satisfied with what he saw. He knew it would give nothing away. Mysteries like this never did, not at first glance. And he was right.

Staring off into the gully, he watched it run for a few hundred yards north and then dogleg to the right and disappear. There were some hidden spots. Grown up spots or clumps of trees that let in no light. But most of it was open, partially anyway, and he could tell nothing. He walked the road carefully thirty yards to the left and the same to the right. Nothing. But when he looked straight ahead over the slight incline, he noticed a bare spot near some small pines and a turkey oak. Then, straining his eyes, what could possibly be another bare spot, even bigger or longer than the first, a good ways off.

"Alright then," he said nodding to himself. There was an uncomfortableness stirring now in the base of his stomach. He picked up the radio.

"Hey guys?"

A slight pause.

"What's up," came the bored monotone. How they could lose interest in just under thirty minutes was beyond him. Maybe they hadn't inspected the whole place like they were supposed to. Maybe they wrote it off as third-rate vandalism and smoked a few while they waited for him.

"There's a trail out here. It's... uh, well... I'm not sure what to make of it right yet." There was a pause as he thought not only about what he would do next, but what to tell the guys. If he decided to head off like a bloodhound through the woods, it would be smart to have the guys swing around. It could, after all, actually *be* a gang of crazed Satanists. Backup would be nice. But then calling for backup was also making him feel a little like he was admitting he was freaked out. Like he needed that light on and the TV going before he could go to sleep without Mommy or Daddy in the room. But that was silly. Having the guys take the time to drive around made sense, even if they were bored to death and ready to high tail it back to the station. Ben knew they got off in a couple of hours, and he didn't want to be the one to force overtime on a wild goose chase, or dog chase for that matter.

"Hey, look guys. I need you to come around where I'm at. I'm going to follow this trail around the bend here and see what's up. It looks like they drug the dogs off deep in the woods."

A mildly tentative voice, "Into the woods? No sign of a truck or nothing?"

"Nah, just some early drinker heading to a cabin back in here. Harmless though." He thought about mentioning the dead dog in the back of the guy's SUV, but that would have raised more questions, and Ben wasn't much for radio rhetoric.

"Alrightee... how do we get there?"

*****

Dan had almost run off the road twice. Once because he was so engrossed in the rearview mirror. He had slipped off the edge of the road and taken down a small sapling no bigger around than the size of his thumb. He jerked the truck back into the middle of the road and cursed the tree as he heard it slide down the front grill and tickle the underside of his truck.

Only two more bends in the road, and I'm at the cabin turnoff.

A fifty-yard straight-line trek, two or three quick beers on the porch, and he would be ready to chunk Charlie. No sense in wasting energy. Karen would never dig him up. He would break the ground up a little and then tie a couple of cinder blocks to him and watch his troublesome ass sink to the bottom of the lake.

The second time he lost control, he almost careened down the side of a ravine. Driving thirty miles an hour on an old, unkempt road was not entirely intelligent, even in a time of stress. When the Jimmy humped it over a raised oak root that spanned the road, Dan's hands had momentarily left the steering wheel, and the truck had lurched left. For an added panic, the gun on the seat bounced up and landed in the floor, barrel pointing directly at Dan's feet. So, after his head bounced off the roof of the cab, and as his body began its way down to the seat, Dan could already see the outcome. The Nine would land and discharge a nice, hot piece of lead through both of his ankles. He would be unable to step on the brake, the Jimmy rollercoastering down the side of the mountain with his soon-to-be dead body flailing helplessly behind the wheel.

The gun, however, did not go off. But he still brought both knees up as high as he could on each side of the steering wheel, looking like a Cirque de Soleil outcast about to die of shock. When he finally got his foot to the brake, he was katty-cornered just off the edge of the road with one tire slipping in the mud, slowing tilting the truck down the side of the mountain. He quickly slammed it in reverse as the Jimmy decided it didn't care to tackle the tree studded incline, either.

The beer that had been resting cozily between his legs was now in the floor and most of the frothing liquid was spread across the front of his pants and dripping down his legs. He sat in the middle of the road for a moment, trying to calm down. The smell of the beer went from soothing to irritatingly rancid. His hand and leg were throbbing anew, and the gun was still pointing at his ankles.

He peered down the last stretch of road. One last bend to go. Surely he could make it the last fifty fucking yards to the turn without killing himself. He bent over and picked up the gun, flicking the safety back on as he tossed it into the passenger's seat. He didn't even glance at the can in the floor. Screw it. He could feel the wound on his leg, slightly moistening again. That he ignored, too. There was one thing that was out of place though that bothered him more than anything. The rearview mirror was crooked and showing nothing more than passenger's side floorboard.

You heard it didn't you, Danny boy? It was in the chaos of the moment, but you heard it anyway didn't you. That small bit of rustling from the back seat. Like a playful bit of plastic come to life?

He moved his right arm slowly up to the rearview and twisted it around. His heart had sped up during his psuedo-crash, and now it was racing, thundering down the track like a drag racer with a flat tire. If Charlie was behind him, he would have to be quick in grabbing the gun. And with his head stiff and facing the rearview, he couldn't remember what position the gun was lying in. He couldn't afford to fumble around, not now. The dog back on the interstate flashed in his head for some insane reason and he tensed every muscle in his body as the reflection swung around.

Nothing.

Dan exhaled.

Then he slowly swung his head around just to make sure and looked over the back of his seat to check the floor. He checked the position of the gun for good measure. Barrel toward the door and lying on its left side for a perfect grab in case of emergency. He pulled forward cautiously.

Keep your head, Dan. Je-sus.

The turn was finally here, marked by a solitary mini-boulder that resembled one of those Stone Henge thingies. Why all people with money wanted boulders in their yard, he just couldn't figure. Forty yards of pebble-sized gravel led down to a small opening that served as a parking area for both the Bowers' cabin and, a ways off to the right, the Bigsbys' cabin. His light at the end of this crazy day's tunnel was the cabin to the left.

It was a quaint piece of Heaven with one bathroom, one bedroom, a living room/kitchen/dining room, and a screened-in porch. The porch rested just above the start of the hill that ran down to the lake, not twenty yards below. He could see the top of the first stone step that led a hand-laid pathway down to the boat dock. The spilt beer was beginning to take on more of a sumptuous bouquet now that he was within reach of the other eight.

He turned to check on his little red and white buddies in the next seat when something caught his eye in the rearview. He looked up and saw Charlie staring back at him.

Everything that was Dan shut down.

His mind blanked. His body a lump of catatonic tumbleweed. The neurons that were firing were a blind army of frightened, untrained misfits. Charlie's misshapen snout, from what Dan could see in the mirror, couldn't be more than an inch from his right ear.

Why can't I feel his breath?

Then there was a blur of movement.

8

"We're going to the fair. Put on something skimpy."

"To the what?"

Karen had a wild slice of smile going on and a look of determination that would have sent the Titanic straight through an iceberg without slowing down.

"Something tells me you're not going to be using the Ferris wheel for therapy. You sure you're okay? Do I need to bring a gun or hand grenade or something?"

"Nope," Karen smiled. "Just a smile and a wink."

With that Karen got up and went to the guest room. Carol supposed she was changing.

"Okay then, girl. I gotcha back."

Carol got up and walked to her room, slightly excited. Her friend was looking vengeful, and rightfully so. She had that same feeling she'd had when she was fourteen and about to roll Bobby Stephen's house down the street.

9

The side of his head exploded with pain. He shot forward, his chest hitting the steering wheel, making the horn wail momentarily. He could feel his body slam into something and stop, but even in the chaos, he could feel his ear being held in a pair of vice grips. He screamed to no one. He kept screaming as he heard a sickening sound. Part of his ear had given up the fight, and the tearing sound was in slow motion. He had no way of knowing how much of his ear had been ripped away, but the sound was horrific. As a gut reaction, he lifted his right arm to block the attack.

He felt an immediate warmness on his shoulder and the top of his arm. Then the teeth sinking into his armpit, hard. Like a crocodile had been loosed in the vehicle.

So powerful.

Dan slung his body against the left door and his head slammed against the driver's window as he attempted, through blood and panic, to find the door handle with his left hand. But his left arm was tangled up in a spider's web of steering wheel. His screams were now high-pitched from pure terror. As the liquid fire leaked from his right ear and crushing jaws sunk deeper still into his armpit, Dan feared he would pass out from the pain.

They will never know what happened.

The Jimmy had left the road and plowed its way through some sapling pines before heading up the incline to the left of the road. The truck bounced a few times as it hit rocks and small trees. Dan's ass suddenly left the seat as his head cocked sideways, slamming into the ceiling of the Jimmy. The grip on his arm wasn't there anymore. Dan remembered the gun in the seat. As the SUV made its way up the hill, the weight of the vehicle naturally caused it to turn back down the incline and bounce onto the road again.

Dan lowered his arms so he could see and turned his head to find an empty seat. The gun had fallen from the seat. He caught the sight of it from the corner of his eye as Charlie came over the back seat and snapped his teeth together on Dan's scalp. Someone was driving nine inch landscaping nails through his skull. The canines stopped only when they hit bone, then slid off and found purchase on skin and hair.

Dan dove for the gun in the passenger's floorboard, his head cocking backwards with Charlie attached to it. Charlie was up front with him now, and as Dan's crumpled form hit the floorboard, Charlie's feet were planted on Dan's back and the seat. Dan could feel the gun pressing into his collar bone as he tried to move his hands around again in close quarters. Then suddenly, quickly, the gun was in his right hand. But he was trapped face down in the floorboard and Charlie had him by the backside of his head. He could feel Charlie shaking his head side to side, a playful mutt who didn't want to let go of his toy, playing tug-o-war with his owner. But in this case, the toy was Dan's head.

His opportunity to turn around came as Charlie shook back and forth again, Dan's head following suit, his teeth gritting, and a piece of his scalp peeled off into Charlie's mouth. The tearing and ripping sound again. His vision blurred for a second and Dan wasn't sure he could take any more pain. He spun around to shoot and in the panic, pulled the trigger too soon, *before* he had turned a full 180 degrees, and almost blew off his own face. Charlie didn't seem to mind as a tight little hole appeared in the ceiling of his Jimmy. Then Dan was around. Arm bent crooked and funny looking, but turned around just the same. Charlie dropped the hair and came for him again. Dan emptied the pistol. He could see a few chunks of Charlie hit the ceiling and the force of the bullets threw the dog over the seat.

After a few useless clicks of the pistol, Dan's finger stopped and he stared wild-eyed at a ceiling full of holes. Then at the front seat. If Charlie came back over the seat, he was out of ammo. He was fucked. No way out. No way, no how.

Get up, Dan. Get up!

He was screaming to himself on the inside. On the outside all he could hear was the sound of gravel and …

The SUV tilted and Dan realized, for the first time since he had looked in the rearview mirror, where he was. He was in the floor of the Jimmy and the Jimmy had just made its way down the gravel driveway to the drop off that ran down to the boathouse… and the lake.

*****

If Officer David Lackey would have turned his head and looked at his partner, he would have seen a strange site on Lake Cleburne that day. About three hundred yards to his left, across the lake, he would have seen a white Jimmy bouncing its way down the side of a hill. But Lackey just wasn't the kind of person who had to look you in the face while he was talking to you. He might be brushing a spot of mud from his shoe or watching the sky like it was about to deliver a long-awaited sign from Heaven. Anything but giving you conversational validation. Maybe it was his way of rebelling against all those high school teachers that demanded his constant focus.

Instead of seeing the rather large splash in the distance, they both continued talking about how they should be fishing on that lake right now instead of running around in the woods looking for some idiot teenagers who were long gone. They talked about how all these rich fuckers had houses on the lake that cost more than they could make in ten years. They talked about everything except the job they were doing at present and that helped a little to ease the pain of work.

*****

Gravity, his crumpled position in the floorboard, the tilt of the Jimmy, and the springing up and down as the vehicle careened down the embankment, all contributed to Dan remaining helplessly in the floor on his back as the SUV smacked the water. He could feel the Jimmy slide out into the lake like a waterlogged piece of driftwood. Immediately, the water sifted its way to the interior. Dan's bloody head slammed against the underside of the glove compartment and for a split second everything went black.

His ears rang and he felt his head go underwater. There was no chance for preparation. He hadn't braced himself or held his breath. Water had entered his mouth and as he flailed like a drunken flamingo inside the sinking Jimmy, the water that had snuck into his mouth slipped down his throat like hot mercury. For a split second, he almost swam for the back of the SUV, for the air pocket. Then he remembered Charlie.

He's in here with you. Wet and bloody and dead.

If Dan could have screamed underwater, he would have. Instead, he found the door handle on the left side and began jerking it to no avail. His eyes wide with panic, he could already feel the lightness in his head and the tightness in his chest as the absence of oxygen formed a hollow cavity of despair behind his sternum. He pulled himself closer to the door. It was almost impossible to see in the greenish, muddy water.

The lock! The lock!

He flipped it. Jerked again. The door moved outward, much slower than he wanted. He pressed his feet against the seat and waved his arms in wide chaotic arcs.

Then, finally… air.

He gasped as the air and water mixed in his mouth and throat. Dan was choking and coughing and trying to take in only the air and sift out the water that was trying to kill him. Dan's feet finally found purchase in a soft and squishy bottom near the bank. He drug himself to the edge and collapsed, half in and half out of the water. He lay there for a good three minutes, left side of his face in the mud, before he could breathe normally without a fit of coughing.

He's behind you, Danny Boy.

Dan peeled his face from the mud and looked back at the water.

Nothing.

Only the slight remnants of ripples headed for the other side of the lake and a ghostly pale image three or so feet under the water, about fifteen feet out. But the bottoms of his legs were still in the water, and he didn't like that one bit. He forced himself to stand. He suddenly felt just how alone he really was in the world. There weren't many people on the lake right now. As he looked around the banks at the four houses within sight, none of them looked active. No cars. No boats on the lake. No one around at all. Just him and no vehicle and…

His gun was in the car. So was his cell phone. He looked across the lake to the spill way where Lackey and Wheels had just driven past. But there was nothing there now, and as far as Dan was concerned, there might never be. If he took the road to the front entrance, the one that most people used during their weekend trips, it was a forty-five minute walk at best.

I didn't close the door.

It was a silly thought. Especially since, at the time, he was drowning. But to Dan it would have been a little more unnerving, not much, but a little, if he had just found a second or two to close that door. But it was down there in the murk and moss, open. He stared at the calm water for a minute. If anyone had just appeared on the bank, he would have never known the chaos that just ensued.

And if someone drives by, or for that fact, even if someone comes around the bend tossing lures at the bank, he will never know I'm in trouble.

And he was in trouble. With a capital fucking *T.* He could feel Karma coming down on him like Dorothy's farm house. He had screwed around on his wife on the kitchen table that had taken them three months to decide on. He had killed her dog and was going to throw it over a bridge and be done with it. And just five minutes ago he had planned to have a few beers and then tie a block to Charlie and sink him to the bottom of the lake.

And the beer. The damn beer is in the car.

Another stupid thought to have.

And here was the truth of it. A truth that his mind had tried to flee from, to hide in the bushes from. But this truth chased him down. It sunk its claws in his side and made him believe whether he liked it or not.

Charlie was dead.

Charlie was dead before he left the house. Charlie was dead on the way here as he lay stinking in the back of the Jimmy, wrapped in plastic. Charlie was dead when he was staring at Dan in the rearview, gnarled teeth and half-skinned face no more than an inch from Dan's. Charlie was dead in the water, so to speak, at this very moment. Yes, Charlie was dead, but that hadn't stopped him so far. And although Dan couldn't see him behind that glassy reflection of the lake, he was right there below him. Not a horseshoe's toss away.

Dead.

And dead suddenly seemed to take on a new meaning to the Danmeister. Dead was now more or less a relative term. A state of mind. A decision of the will, maybe. Hell, maybe he couldn't define it like old Webster, but he knew one thing for certain. Dead wasn't what it used to be. Dead wasn't what it was supposed to be. Dead had crawled itself up from somewhere dark and hot and slithered its way into a drizzly, overcast day at Lake Cleburne.

It's just a matter of time now, Danny.

He didn't like the path that his mind was headed down so he drug his exhausted body from the muddy embankment and started limping towards the boat house. It was only ten or so yards to the left. The out of control Jimmy could have easily slammed into the boathouse and made a hell of a mess. But no. No evidence on this scene. As he reached the natural stone steps that led up the hill to the cabin, his senses rushed back and he was once again aware of his body. His leg, hand, armpit, head, and ear. Sharp pains and dull pains mixed together like a hellish biological cocktail. He remembered the tearing sounds and his stomach weakened again at the thought.

He brought his hand to his ear and winced in pain as he touched the open wound. He wasn't even going to put his hand to his head, afraid of what he might feel. He took one more look over his shoulder and proceeded up the stairs, body aching with every step. He was exhausted.

The key. The key is on the key chain. In the ignition. In the Jimmy. Great.

But he knew the spare was next to the front door, lying under a concrete turtle. And he also knew that there was liquor in the cabinets. Her dad's *Gentlemen's Jack*. He wasn't much for bourbon, but right now it sounded like Heaven. Dripping, soaked to the gills, he reached the third step from the top and heard something below.

Dan didn't want to look. He wanted to ignore it and then it would surely go away. Because surely this nightmare was over.

He turned and saw Charlie standing just out of the water. The top of his head looked like it had exploded. Two big chunks missing on his shoulder and side. But the head was worse than before. Now it wasn't just skin from his jowls rolled up and exposing the side of his teeth and face. Now it was the top of his head looking like a wet, crimson volcano of flesh. Dan knew the hollow point bullet had done it. Left a much larger hole on the way out than it made on the way in, because that's the way they were designed. But his thoughts were getting a little murky, kind of like the water in the lake that his wife's dead dog had just crawled out of.

Too long in the microwave. Popped like a chicken egg.

Dan started to move slowly towards the top step, like a mime in slow motion, caught in invisible quicksand. Charlie just stood there, head slightly cocked.

No, it was Pop Rocks. Pop Rocks and then he drank Coke. And boom! There goes the top of his little doggy head.

He kept his gaze on Charlie and moved his legs to the next step. One more to go. And then he could surely make it twenty feet to the key and get in the cabin before Charlie got up the hill. Slowly, slowly. Almost home. He glanced down at his foot so he wouldn't trip up at the finish line and then back up at Charlie. He could literally feel the blood making its way down the side of his face. Everything was in slow motion. He could feel the blood's thickness as it trickled down past his cheek and dripped from his jaw. Both feet were now on the top step. He could make it now for sure.

Dan turned to run for the turtle and stopped dead.

The parking area in front of him was a wide open graveled space about the size of a baseball infield. To his left was the next door neighbor's timber-framed two story. Almost directly in front of him and to the right was the cabin.

Scattered throughout the parking area, and disappearing into the woods behind it, were over a hundred dogs.

None of them looked alive.

They all looked very dead.

But then again, Dan thought, *dead isn't what it used to be.*

10

Jean Hutz listened to Karen with a few "uh-huh's" and "okay's" and then asked her where her car was. Well, she'd said, it wasn't exactly her car. Then she told him whose car it was and that he could blame her if the police came knocking and that she would pay him $300.00 wife-free money. Even though he wasn't married, Jean knew that wife-free money meant your wife never had to know about it. It would be a nice wad of cash he could use to visit the Pink Oyster down on Hwy 78. Sometimes when the girls at the Pink Oyster gave you a lap dance in a side room, they gave you a little preview of what was available for a bigger wad of cash. This was definitely a bigger wad of cash.

So, since Jean had known Karen since junior high, and since he had always had a slight crush on her, and since he had worked with one of the dancers at the Pink Oyster in a five and dime once and really wanted to see her butt-ass naked again, he said *yes*. Why the hell not?

Karen and Carol headed to the hardware store downtown. After they made their purchase, Carol started to get a little nervous. She tried not to show it, but Karen picked up on her hesitation.

"Don't worry," Karen reassured her best friend. "It's not going to be us using them."

That didn't necessarily make Carol feel any better about the situation. But she had Karen's back 'til the bitter end. Her friend deserved this little bit of retribution, even if they both spent the night in jail.

"And," Karen added enthusiastically, "It might even make us a few hundred!"

Carol helped sling the sledge hammers into the back of the car. Now she was slightly interested. How in the world could they make a few grand off destroying this slut's car? And where in the world, she asked herself, could they get away with this without anybody seeing them. And Karen explained that everybody would see them. Then they would help them. And they would pay to do it.

Carol was hooked.

11

The turtle suddenly seemed very far away. Could he reach it?

Maybe.

Probably.

But that was if these things, *and what were they exactly*, ran at the same speed as normal dogs, *normal* meaning *alive*. If so, he could probably reach the key. But then what?

They would be only a few feet away by then, and he would be standing at the door and fumbling with the lock like they always do in horror flicks. No good. The only other door was in the back. A small screened in porch with a little screen door and then a short little four feet or so to the back door. It was probably dead-locked, but maybe he could use the screen door to keep them out while he crawled through a window.

Could he make the back door? Sure. If he didn't stumble on the uneven and rocky ground. Would the screen door be locked? Was there something to use as a weapon on the little porch in the back . . . wicker chair, glass table, plants and . . .

All this passed through Dan's mind in less than a second. And a good thing, too, because as soon as that second was up, every dog in the parking area came at him.

He turned and sprinted as fast as he could along the lake-facing side of the cabin. To his left was the underside of the second, and more grandiose, screened-in porch that sat on stilts and overlooked the lake. To his right a couple of feet was the start of a gradual incline that ran down to the lake. Behind him, Hell . . . behind him he couldn't even think about. Could not fathom. His mind didn't have enough room left for pondering what type of Hell Pack was on his heels. He was in survival mode. Every Dan cell was working to get inside the cabin and put a wall of brick and wood between whatever these things were and himself. To hell with the rest.

He could hear an insane number of feet pounding behind him as he rounded the corner and slung open the screen door. It wasn't locked. One for the Dan Team. He shoved it closed and locked it. Turning quickly, he tried the door handle to the cabin just to make sure. Locked. Then he heard the aluminum on the screen door shake. He spun around, in the process his eyes scanning the corner of the space for a weapon, and saw parts of the screen give way. Teeth gnawing viciously at the frail door. The tiny latch would not hold long. Dan knew he only had a second before the door gave. When a ripping sound drew his attention to his right, he looked down to see a large set of canines ripping madly into what looked like a small mouse hole. The mouse hole was widening.

In the opposite corner, he saw what appeared to be a miniature gardening shovel and one of those three pronged thingies for raking the dirt around. No good. He needed a Gatlin gun, not fucking gardening equipment. One of the ornamental aluminum pieces bent inward as a set of teeth found its way four or five inches through the door.

Dan was already panicked. Now he panicked on top of panicking. He screamed like an idiot at the dog as loudly as he could manage. If you would have asked him a few seconds later what he had said he wouldn't have remembered. He reached up and pressed his bloody hands against the window and tried to lift it up from the outside. Locked. More ripping. Dan felt like crying.

There was no time to cry. There was no time to think. There was only time to do. And so Dan was about to break the window out, even though it was chest high and not really big enough for him to fit through, if he could find a chair to stand on.

He stopped. Something behind him. He spun around and saw what had crawled through the tiny opening that was being ripped wider as he stood there.

Bug-eyed. Ears back. Teeth bared. Toes painted.

There was a slight decay to this one, but not bad. Whatever grave this one came from wasn't years old. A few months maybe. The pale coat was filthy with mud and the little chameleon eyes were glazed over with a nasty white film. To go with the pink toes was a pink doggie vest. Dan wanted to bust out laughing but was so horrified that all he could manage was an ineffectual lisp of a smile. He thought about grabbing the mini-garden shovel and chopping the little fucker in half, but the thought of even coming close to the Night-of-the-Living-Dead Chihuahua made his skin literally crawl. The bottom of the screen door buckled and the little Chihuahua darted for him.

Dan grabbed the glass top table and pulled it over with all he could manage. As the glass shattered in front of the charging dog, Dan turned and kicked, as hard as any policeman on TV had ever kicked, at the back door. Perhaps if the door had originally been installed to swing in, instead of out, Dan's Hawaii Five-O kick would have worked. As it were, his leg slammed directly through the two thin sheets of plywood that made up the back door.

His leg jammed forward and lodged itself, past the knee, into the door. There was a scraping of paws behind him as the table turned all the way over and the legs poked up in the air. Dan placed his hands on the door and pushed with all his might. He screamed in pain for the umpteenth time today as splinters slid into the meat of his leg on the way out. Another pain as the little tike sunk its tiny teeth into his ankle. Dan screamed like an idiot once more and kicked the dog hard enough to send it into the far wall.

Now the hole in the wall the Chihuahua came through was almost big enough for a medium sized dog to fit through and by the looks of it, one was on its way. He knelt down and shoved his left arm through the hole in the door and felt for the deadbolt. Thank God it wasn't keyed on both sides. He turned the latch and then felt for the lock on the door handle itself. Twisting it to the horizontal position, he jerked his arm out through the hole, slung the door open and slammed it shut.

Dan latched the deadbolt and locked the doorknob as well. He was in. He leaned against the door and let out a small sigh of relief. Then he screamed again in pain. He reached for his pants leg and was able to rip it away, some of the pants and a little bit of the skin coming off as teeth gnashed through the hole he had made with his leg. Like a dunce, he had his leg against the door when he leaned on it to take a breath. Now it was another spot on him that was bleeding.

He left the door and ran into the kitchen. He pulled out drawers like a cat burglar ransacking a house. He found what he was after and ran back to the door where the dog's snout was feeling for another bit of Dan flesh through the hole. Dan raised the meat cleaver above his head and came down as hard as he could. As the dog's snout fell to the floor, Dan looked down at it with a morbid curiosity. There was still thrashing at the door. He looked at the hole and saw what looked like a high school dissection gone awry. It was a clear cut-away of the dog's snout, like something from a medical journal sketched in Hell. It was still working at the splintered hole, although there wasn't much to work – like someone's toothless grandma trying to suck a milkshake through the lid without using a straw.

Dan's stomach went queasy. He kicked the severed snout down the short hallway and into a corner. Then it stopped. The sickening half-snout removed itself from the door, and he could hear a lot of footsteps that sounded like they were moving away from the porch. Did he run them off? Did they finally realize they couldn't make it through the door without losing their chops?

He stood to the side of the small hole and listened for a few minutes after the noise outside stopped.

Silence.

That wasn't necessarily a good thing. He crouched down, wincing from the multiple points of pain in his legs, and peered out through the hole, keeping his face a safe distance from the opening. The aluminum door was shredded and hanging mostly off the doorjamb. There were no Hell Hounds out there that he could see, except one.

Charlie.

Charlie was sitting there with his meatloaf brains hanging out, about eight or nine feet outside of the screen door. He was staring at Dan. It was now that Dan noticed his own heavy breathing, and how amazingly exhausted he was.

Charlie did nothing.

He just sat there.

And stared.

The reason Dan noticed that he was breathing so hard was because Charlie wasn't. He had always been active before. Always running, playing, and fetching with Karen. And he had always been panting and slobbering in that thick coat of his. But now there was no panting. His brains and the side of his face were hanging out, but his tongue wasn't.

That's when it occurred to Dan that there was no reason for a dead animal to pant, or slobber, or breathe. Things felt suddenly quiet, and Dan managed to slow his own panting down a bit. It was so loud in the cabin.

Then Dan realized what else it was that had unnerved him so when he was being chased and attacked. The silence. The absolute maddening silence. There was no breathing and so there was no need for barking. No growling. No panting. When Charlie had first attacked him, there had been no initial attack-growl, just the whispery sound of teeth flying through the air and latching on to his ear. And when the other dogs had chased him around the house and had begun chewing and scratching their way into the screened-in porch, there had been only silence then, too. He remembered the sound of the aluminum bending and the wood paneling being ripped apart, but nothing else. It was a disturbing silence. And it made Dan not want to make a sound himself. It made him feel like he was in a library. In the fifth ring of Hell.

And so Charlie sat there motionless and stared through the hole in the door in complete and utter silence.

The fifth ring of Hell, Danny boy. Guess what that means? Four more to go.

12

The little bitch's car was right where she thought it would be. In the parking lot at Dan's work. After the breakup, she called some of their mutual friends and began asking questions. She had gotten an earful. Not from everyone. There were some spoiled little Dan followers who wouldn't spill the beans. There were some who were just uncomfortable with the conversation from the get-go, understandably so, she guessed. But at the time, she hadn't known how long the cheating had been going on, and Karen was trying to squeeze out two things.

One, did any of their so-called friends know about this and not say anything? If so, they could piss off. She would cut that tie in a heartbeat. And she did just that with Kimberly and Jason. Nice enough couple; and although they weren't lying when they said they didn't know anything, she felt like they were holding *something* back. So she was done with them. *Par-a-noi-a strikes deep*, she thought.

Two, how long had she been an idiot? How long had he been screwing this whore right there on the table where they ate dinner? But she answered that question as soon as she asked it. She had been an idiot since she had said, "I do."

One little morsel of information had now proven very useful. She worked overtime. Good thing this wasn't one of those big corporations with fenced-in parking lots and a guard at the gate. This was wide open, and there were only about seven or eight other cars in the parking lot. There were no people and the traffic on Walnut Avenue was minimum. Everyone was taking Bynum-Cutoff to the fair.

She was getting a little skittish now, standing here and waiting on Hutz.

"Okay. You know I love you, right?" Carol was looking nervously around.

"Stop fidgeting, soldier. If she comes out, we'll gang her prison style. K?"

"I'm fine, I'm fine. It would just be nice if Hutz came on with it. You know?"

"I know."

They both leaned on the hood of Carol's car and waited. And waited. Five minutes felt like fifty.

"You know what this is like?" Carol finally asked, breaking the silence.

"What?"

"It's like bank robbers showing up outside the bank with their masks on and their guns drawn and then just standing there for a half hour until they rob the bank."

"Pretty much. Call it moxie. Dillinger had moxie. All the really good bank robbers have moxie."

Carol was pretty sure that her BFF had gone batty. Two weeks ago, she would have never thought Karen had the balls to pull something this spectacular. Now she was nervously wondering just how big those balls had grown. But all the same, she was glad to see her finally taking action. It would help her feel better. It would help her heal.

A rusty bucket of bolts came flying around the corner and into the parking lot. Hutz didn't even stop for hello's. He made an oval pattern and backed the truck right in front of the target. Hopping out, he gave a jogging curtsy to the ladies and began moving the knobs on the side of the truck. Hutz moved rather nimbly for such a jolly-sized man, raking out the chains and looping them somewhere under the car.

As the car began to slide slowly up the inclined ramp, Jean Hutz looked over and smiled at Karen and Carol. Partners in crime. They smiled evil, little knowing smiles back. Then Sheryl walked out of the building.

Jean's hand wavered for a second at the controls, and the car came to a halt about a third the way up the ramp. His eyes wide with uncertainty.

Carol said, under her breath to Karen, "Oh, shit. Now what?"

Karen said nothing, and just crossed her arms and stared at Sheryl as she walked toward them, eyeing the tilted car and the people standing around it.

Sheryl looked like she was about to ask what the hell was going on when she seemed to recognized Karen. She stopped about ten feet from Hutz's rig and just stared at all of them, being careful to avoid Karen's eyes. No one said a word for 10 whole seconds, an interminable period under the circumstances. Then Sheryl walked around the front side of the rig, avoiding Karen and Carol, right past Hutz with his hand still frozen on the control and walked right up the ramp.

She opened the door with her key and, with the weight of the door leaning on her, reached into the car and pulled out a bag and another set of keys. She reached up and grabbed her cd's from the visor, then let the door swing shut. Without a word or second glance, Sheryl walked down the ramp, around the front of the tow truck, and headed back to the double doors she had emerged from.

Carol and Hutz continued with their daydream as Karen opened the door to Carol's car.

Karen said, "Well, c'mon. Posse up, bitches."

Hutz and Carol stared wide-eyed at the crazy lady getting behind the wheel. She was apparently losing her mind. And so they slowly followed suit.

13

Ben could feel the wetness sinking into his underwear. A copper smudge on his ass and left side marking the fall he had on the way down the slope. The leaves turned out to be a natural slip and slide, and the small pine sapling hadn't held his weight.

He was about two hundred yards from the road when Lackey and Wheels pulled up in front of his car. He could still see them in the distance, getting out of the car and milling around, looking lost in general. They were looking his way but probably couldn't see him. The valley floor was thick in this area with brambles and ivy and even a little clump of bamboo that he thought was weirdly out of place. He took out his cell phone.

"Hello?" said Wheels. Had a cell phone now for over a year and still couldn't figure out how to set the voicemail message or figure out who was calling by the ring.

"It's Ben," he said. "I'm about two hundred yards or so south of you guys. Seen a few clumps of hair here and there and following the trail on into the woods. You two hang tight in case I need you."

"Roger that."

Wheels sounded like he had stayed up all night studying for a midterm. Couldn't really blame them for wanting to get off on time, could he?

Ben walked another fifty yards before he lost the trail. He was no Pocahontas, and it would take him another 20 minutes to find it on the other side of the small creek.

*****

Dan the man, now Dan-the-bleeding-profusely-man, sat in front of the fireplace in the room that contained the kitchen, living room, and dining room all in one. He stared up at the large oak beams that spanned the roof and wondered how much it cost to have them placed there. How much does a beam that damn big set a fellow back?

He thought these thoughts because they were a welcome stand-in for the only other thoughts available to him at the moment. Thoughts of zombie-like animals that have this little, slightly remote lakeside cottage surrounded. As his blood soaked into the couch where he lay slumped like a wet sack of potatoes, the fire he had started offered hypnotic relief. You can always count on a campfire or fireplace to suspend the senses. Something about staring through the flames while they lick at the air and then just perish for their trouble. Something about performing the same kind of primal act that cavemen had been acting out for millennia, that gave the mind reprieve from the troubles of survival. And that is what Dan was trying very hard to do at the moment. Survive.

The first twenty minutes, he had run through the house like a wounded banshee and taken every piece of furniture that was not nailed down and placed it in front of the only two doors in the cottage. Then he had used a hammer and nailed the doorjambs to the doors and even a couple of chair legs to the floor after setting them in front of the door. They weren't getting in unless they could fly through windows that were a good six feet off the ground. But what wasn't possible here?

He could see their claws sinking into the vinyl that rested just above the outside brick. The dead muscles contracting as they pulled themselves up the side of the cottage like overgrown, mutated alien spiders. No, no, no. Back to the fire. Just stare at the fire Dan and let your mind rest for a second or two. He breathed deeply and began to do something he hadn't done in years.

Dan began crying. He hated himself for it, but could not stop. It was just all too much. A divorce on the horizon, a torn up bumper, probably a pint of blood strewn here and there, and a now a Pack of the Dead waiting for him outside. He had lost his cell phone and when he had tried to dial out, the phone rang three times and went dead right as 911 had picked up. The dogs could have easily chewed through the wire. He sure as hell wasn't about to go stick his head out the bathroom window and check.

His only solace was the vodka, tequila, and Jack Daniels he had found in the bottom cabinet. Top shelf. Karen's dad had a taste for liquor, and a good one at that. Screw the beer. This fifth of vodka was three-quarters full and the Jose Cuervo was only half empty, or maybe half full, depending on your outlook. Dan's outlook was, like his vision, very blurry at the moment. He stared into the fire and wondered what would happen if he just threw the tequila bottle in the fire and ran for the boats down by the lake while the cottage burned to the ground. Surely that would bring help. He could just sit in the boat in the middle of the lake until someone came. They couldn't swim could they?

That's when he heard the knock at the door.

14

A breaded and impaled weenie was being dipped in a careful alchemy of mustard and ketchup as Karen passed by a family of six on her way to the ticket man. A scant supply of plywood and two by fours, painted bright yellow and red, served as a ticket booth. Karen smiled and asked for the man in charge. She was waved to a group of three trailers at the edge of the fairgrounds.

Carol and Hutz nervously watched her disappear in a thicket of cotton candy, stuffed animals, and neon necklaces. Carol glanced at the sky and silently hoped for another small downpour like they'd had this morning. That would maybe ruin the fair and Karen would give up and dump the car in a lake or something. Her wishful thinking was crushed when Karen appeared around the corner and waved Hutz to another entry on the "back side" of the fair.

Thirty minutes later, a rather nice looking Honda Accord sat at the edge of the fairgrounds, saddled in between a loop-de-loop and a ring toss (4 tosses for a dollar, ten tosses for 2 dollars.) As promised, Karen paid the young boy $50, cash-in-hand, for watching over the car and then stepped back to admire the paint job. It was a nice shade of purple, and unlike her own car, which seemed to attract other people's doors and runaway shopping carts, it didn't seem to have a dent anywhere in sight.

That was about to change.

The people were already waiting in line, but the young boy, adept at his line of work, began immediately explaining that the first person would be $20 and not the regular 5 hits for $10. But to Karen's amazement, there were 3 people with hands raised; and, when it was all said and done, a young construction worker had placed the highest bid and laid hands on the sledgehammer for a whopping $50.

Karen understood now why the old man in the trailer had argued with her about the first smack. It was a privilege he knew would draw a little extra cash, and so the conditions were set that she would pay the wages of the person running it and not get first whack. She would also be responsible for clean up later. She was fine with all these terms. She had planned on the carnies paying her some money for the car, but that's not the way carnies work. The whole thing would end up costing her close to half a week's wages, but it was well worth it as she watched the stout fellow climb to the top of the car, smile, and proudly bring down the hammer into the windshield.

Even Carol and Hutz were a little giddy now, both smiling away and shaking their heads side to side in unison. Before the hour was up, Karen had paid for all of them to take some swipes at the Honda themselves. Hutz seemed fixated on the back lights. Carol, though slightly squeamish about the whole thing, held the hammer like it was about to explode and lightly banged on the side door. Karen got her sadistic pleasure from taking a smaller hammer to the nice factory radio inside the car. Her last smash was the rearview mirror.

When they left at around 3:00, they decided to go and have a few margaritas at the Frontera Mexican Restaurant. They laughed as they poured through the digital pictures that Carol had taken and Hutz told Karen to, "Remind me never to piss you off!"

"I owe you a big one," Karen told Hutz with a flirtatious, half-drunken smile.

Hutz's mind wondered with delight at the possibilities.

15

Dan was startled, but came to with the alarm of a hibernating bear. He wasn't three sheets to the wind yet, but he was two sheets at least. The bottle dropped from his hand, and he had to bend over in a hurry to keep the sideways bottle from leaking out all the good stuff.

Was that a knock? Or had he dreamed it?

Bam! Bam! Bam!

The front door!

"Hey!" was all he could manage, stumbling wildly for the door. But the door was blocked by an array of broken furniture and didn't have a window in it. He ran to the side window and looked slantingly out to see a uniformed officer. In fact, it looked like the same cop that had almost busted him on the back road.

"Officer Ben Braswell." A commanding voice. "May I speak with you, please."

It didn't sound like a question, but Dan didn't quite know what to do.

"Hold on a second."

His options reeled through his mind like the first cut of a bad B Movie. He looked out of all the windows to make sure the dogs were gone before opening the door. That might take too long or seem suspicious. Or worst case, the dogs were already coming for the cop. What would a clip with nine bullets or so do against a canine army of the dead? This officer was a link, though, to the outside world. Didn't they always carry a walkie-talkie or something, a cell phone surely? If the dogs got him, his link would be broken, gone forever, dead and bloody, not two feet in front of the door and Dan with no way to get out of his own prison. But if he opened the door, then the officer would see all the shit piled in front of the door and think he was a lunatic. But so what?

He felt like a lunatic.

Dan grabbed a hammer and started yanking nails out by the heads.

"Sir, are you alright?" The voice from outside. Outside the prison.

"Just fine. Remodeling. *What a stupid thing to say*! Hold on!"

Nails screeching their way out of the doorjamb; chairs and cutting boards scattering across the floor. Dan was deconstructing his rendition of the *Close Encounters of the Third Kind* mountain model.

Recognizing the voice from earlier, and hearing a slight tone of panic, Ben backed up and undid, for the second time in the same day, the clip on his holster. He then called Wheels on his cell and told them how to get to the cabin. This wasn't making sense at all. Hope for the best, prepare for the worst. And he could feel the worst coming alright. It was just around the corner.

Finally, the door opened with a cracking of wood and a pair of wild eyes glared out, not at him, but all around him and behind him. It was so unnerving that he ventured to take his eyes off the man for a second and glance behind him.

What the hell is he looking for?

"Jesus Christ almighty! You gotta come in here quick! They're all over the place out there!"

Ben looked up and saw a nail, scraggly and bent, sticking out of the door. He noticed the man's right ear, or what was left of it. He took another step back.

Dan yelled, desperately, "I'm not crazy!"

"Fine, partner. No, problem. Just calm down. Okay."

Dan could see the unclasped holster; the Officer with his hands up in front of him, a placating gesture. Dan scanned the edge of the forest all the way to the other cabin. Nothing. Ben was looking Dan up and down, noticing the wounds all over his body and massive amounts of blood everywhere. Although they wouldn't have time to figure it out, Dan wasn't coming out, and Ben wasn't pushing through a bunch of piled junk to get into the cabin of a lunatic.

"Look," Dan explained as cordially as a man can with a large mix of dried and fresh blood on his clothes. "I know this sounds crazy, but I brought my dead dog up here to bury it because that's what my ex-wife – *Jesus, I just called her Ex* – wanted and then I was attacked by about a hundred dogs. They were trying to get into the house, so I barricaded myself in."

He decided mid-conversation to leave out the part about the dogs being dead. Right now, he needed a little help and help wasn't going to come if he started yammering about Dogs of the Dead.

If it wasn't for a graveyard full of missing dogs, maybe Ben's skin wouldn't have started to crawl. But he needed to assess and control the situation until the others arrived.

"So where are they now?" he questioned.

He watched the madman's eyes wander through the woods. He shook his head in disbelief.

Dan shrugged his shoulders in exasperation. "I don't know."

"You said a hundred?"

"Well... I didn't exactly count 'em while I was being chased, but there were a lot. A lot."

"Okay, so I'm not saying I don't believe you. I'm just asking, where could that many dogs hide that we couldn't see them?"

Dan thought for a moment and then told Ben to hold on, slamming the door.

"Sir! Sir! Please open the door!"

Ben was getting irritated with the whole situation. Was the guy armed? Was he going to get a weapon? He backed up a little more and listened to the other side of the door.

Dan ran as fast as his legs would carry him to the back, bent down, and looked through the hole in the door. Nothing. No Charlie. Not a peep. He ran back to the door and jerked it open. The officer's hand was resting casually on his piece. Dan tried to ignore this. "I didn't see any out back. I don't know... I don't know what's going on."

Ben asked, as he looked around, "Where's your SUV, sir?"

Then it hit Dan. A place where all hundred or so of the dogs could be hiding. He ran across the kitchen area of the cabin and onto the screened in porch. He screamed. It looked more like a thousand now, coming Hell-bent for leather over the edge of the slope that led down to the lake. They had been waiting down there for the right moment. Dan turned in terror as he realized something else. In his panic, he had left the door ajar a good two feet. He ran screaming for the front door.

"Officer! Officer! Look out! To your ri-.."

But Dan could hear the shots from the handgun before he reached the sliding door to the kitchen area. As he crossed the area where the table used to be (it was now in two pieces and boarding up the back door with enough space in the middle for the look-out hole), he could see the officer take multiple hits and fall awkwardly off the side of the stairs while still emptying his gun. He slid to a stop. He wasn't going to make it.

Charlie's mangled face, top of the head mostly gone, slinked around the doorjamb and looked up at Dan.

OmyGodThey'reIN. It's over. There's no way out. None.

But he ran anyway. In his panic, he twisted his ankle as he turned to run and screamed again as he hit the floor, hard. Charlie was on him. The first bite felt like a vice grip. It was unnatural and brutal. He heard the bone splinter inside his flesh and when he crumpled like a child and reached for the thing that was causing all the pain, the thing causing the pain took hold of his hand. Again, bones shattered. Charlie shook his head twice and Dan's hand came off at the wrist. Dan screamed the loudest, most horrible scream he had ever screamed.

Then he shook like an alarm clock and woke up. He was sweating heavily. And nauseous. And the fire was almost out.

*****

Although Ben didn't consider himself out of shape, he hadn't seen the inside of the Ridley Fitness Center in about two years, despite the freebie memberships offered by the owners. Sue and Craig Jacobson sped their BMW and Hummer around Ridley like they were testing the limits of some new jet fighter, and neither one had ever gotten a ticket since they moved there seven years ago. Say what you like. Everybody was happy.

But the heat and humidity from the recent downpour were unbearable. He had fallen twice, feeling like some old man on a TV commercial every time he did. "Help! I've fallen and can't get up!" His pants and the back of his shirt near his ass were soaked and the color of potting soil mixed with some good ole Alabama clay. Lackey and Wheels would have a ball with this one.

Ben was pretty sure that he was climbing slight hills, but they were beginning to feel like mountains. He was walking parallel with the lakeside road. Once, he had even caught a glimpse of it not fifty yards away. But he was still finding patches of hair and bald spots of Earth where the leaves had been drug around by what looked like a huge car-sized rake. So, he decided to stay true to the trail and not lose it after all this work.

His bones were aching, his left foot was killing him (why it chose to start hurting out of the damn blue, he hadn't a clue), and his legs in general felt like loose rubber bands encased in jelly. And he noticed the lengthening shadows. It was a good hour and a half before dark, but the mountains and trees hurried things along when you were in the deep woods. And how long had it taken him to get here? Yeah, probably an hour and a half. If he had been riding in a helicopter, there would have been no question. He would be turning around now.

And in a way, hiking in the woods was like riding in a helicopter. If he got caught fooling around past the halfway mark, and couldn't find his way to the road, then he would be fumbling around in the dark, in the woods. He was having enough trouble navigating by the canopy's twilight. And even if you don't believe in the Boogey Man, you do believe in snakes, mosquitoes, mountain lions, and drop-offs that would land you a broken leg or worse. And then there would be Wheels and Lackey, who would be laughing their asses off while they honked their horns for him to take directions by. And twenty years from now, new deputies would hear the story of how officer Ben Braswell got himself lost in the woods not thirty feet from some dirt road.

But the other option was worse. Losing the mystery. Admitting defeat. Not, as his high school football coach Randy Stevens would have said, leaving it all on the field. Of course, finding some old barn in the middle of the woods full of dead dogs and some crazed, chainsaw-wielding lunatics wasn't something that sounded much better. Especially since it would take God-knew-how-long now for him to call in backup if needed. At least it appeared that if need be, back up could take the road not fifty yards to his right.

Sweat ran over his face and down the back of his neck, soaking his undershirt. As he came over the next hill, a smile creased its way across his exhausted face. It was the road. The main road that they had all come in on, except maybe that guy in the SUV. And directly across from it, a gravel driveway that ran about fifty yards or so around a small bend. Finally. Whoever was responsible, was more than likely here.

He scoured the soaking wet, dirt road in front of him. He could see the recent tracks of their cruisers and a little offset from those, he could see a set of tracks that looked like they disappeared when they got to the gravel driveway. The tracks were not on the left side of the driveway, so that meant it was probably that young fellow he had stopped earlier. He knew that there was something funny about the kid, he just couldn't put his finger on it. What was his name again? Dan something. That was it. And why did he have only one dog in the truck? Did his friends help him out? How many people were down there at the end of this driveway?

He was standing at the top of a small hill with just a smidgeon of underbrush and a few pines. No more than thirty feet from the road. Time to call Wheels and Lackey and have them drive the cruisers around before looking further. Something about the whole layout gave him the willies. He reached down to grab his cell and stopped.

Something had moved to his left, just out of his periphery. He jerked his head sideways and looked into the eyes of a St. Bernard. Except that – and it took his mind a second or two to calibrate – there were no eyes present. Just two sickening hollows of flesh and dirt and, in one place, bone.

It was a large specimen, and its skin seemed to be draped over it like a loose fitting blanket. It was staring at him. But that couldn't be right, because there was no way for it to see. He almost went for his gun, and then decided not to. His mind was racing. An abandoned dog? He had seen some pretty ugly scenes when it came to animal abuse in his years of service, but this would take the cake. But there was... there was... dirt... in the sockets. And the skin was... missing in places. Then the dog turned its head to... look at something?

He turned his head to follow the hollowed-out gaze, not having heard anything himself, and now very cautious with his movements. There were five more dogs of varying sizes that seemed to have emerged from the wet ground like they had been buried just under the leaves. But that didn't make sense, because there wasn't that much space for them to hide. Then he looked at five of the dirtiest, nastiest, horrible-looking canines he had ever seen and realized, finally, what his mind had been trying to tell him since he first saw the St. Bernard. They weren't mistreated and malnourished and on their way to dying. They were already dead.

More movement behind him. He swirled around. Three more. Then behind those, ten more. To his left. More. They seemed to emerge from some two-dimensional space in the very top layer of detritus. Small, medium, and large all clawing their way from the underworld. All in varying stages of decomposition. He was surrounded by what looked like hundreds in less than twenty seconds. He exhaled and realized he had been holding his breath the whole time.

Officer Ben Braswell seemed to have found his mystery at last, and would gladly return it without a receipt and not even ask for the money back. But even in his panic, his training kicked in and his movements were slow, his mind attempting to survey the scene for a way out. He kept his head turning slowly at all times, so as not to be broadsided by any one of them. He definitely needed to call for back up. He definitely needed to draw his weapon. But which one first. The most important was the pistol. Protection. Then the cell phone. Then run. But as he surveyed the surroundings, he realized they were evenly dispersed. There were at least thirty or forty scattered between him and the road below.

His clip held nine bullets.

Ben was afraid, as anyone would be. But he was not screaming in a dead panic and losing control of his faculties in the process. You could blame this on years of discipline and training, on encountering the unexpected as a matter of routine when you were a patrolman, or maybe on all the sci-fi shit he watched and read on a weekly basis. Everything had already been covered in the movies or books. Zombies, aliens, ghosts. Right now Cujo popped into this head, although that dog had been bitten by a bat. And this was most certainly not a rabies problem. Maybe all the movies and magazines had left him slightly immune and unimpressed with the supernatural when he was looking it right in the eye.

But Ben was thinking that it was something else. He was scared shitless, movies or not. But he didn't feel threatened. And why? He noticed that they were all sitting down. They weren't approaching him or circling him. In fact, once they had all emerged from the clay and roots, they hadn't moved a rotting muscle. They were all staring at him. Well, facing would be a better word, since more than half of them didn't have eyeballs, just dirty gray sockets.

Ben's breathing was slow. His eyes darting everywhere. Trying to get a reading.

Something.

But there was nothing.

His body, stiff and unmoving. The decaying dogs all sitting.

They're waiting. I think they're waiting. But for what?

At this point, the fact that they were waiting was a good thing, as far as Ben was concerned. Because what happened when they were finished waiting?

Maybe he should prepare for that moment right about now. His hand moved slightly down to his holster and stopped. He could feel a gentle breeze. He could hear the drops of leftover rain water dripping from the leaves above. Ever so slightly, he grabbed his holster next to the button.

Snap.

It came undone. And every dog that was around him stood up. Soggy leaves fell from their backs.

Okay. Bad idea. Do they know?

They had all moved in unison. Was there some sort of mass awareness here? He moved his hand in place and pushed, hoping that it wasn't the sound of the snap itself that had set them off. If it was, he would have to squeeze off as many shots as possible to make his path to the road. He knew if he had to do that though, that he would never make it. And what then? What would they find in the woods?

Probably nothing. They would tear him to shreds and drag him under the waterlogged leaves and pine straw. There would be nothing but some gun shots that the other officers would hear and another mystery at the end of the day. *Officer still missing as search is called off.*

He held his breath. He pushed on his side.

Snap.

Nothing. For five or six seconds nothing happened. Then, in unison again, they all sat down again. Ben exhaled.

Okay. No drawing the weapon. Fine. How about if I just head back the way I came then fellas?

But the thought of heading back into the darkening woods for a good hour jog didn't seem like a viable option either. That's when all the dogs started moving. The woods were crawling. There were so many of them. By instinct, his hand moved back to his holster. But they weren't approaching him. They were moving in some sort of order that wasn't making sense quite yet. It reminded him of half-time during football games. The band members shuffling in a pattern that didn't make sense until the last second, when they finally made a recognizable design on the field. And the design in front of him now was coming into the light. It was as clear as any decaying beast could make it.

It was a line. Two lines actually. One to his left and one to his right, about ten feet apart. The line led down to the road below at an angle, an angle that Ben realized was pointing away from the driveway ahead and back down the road in the direction of his cruiser. They sat. They did nothing else.

The ones that had not moved to make the line were still scattered haphazardly all over the hillside, all around him. The indication clear. You have one choice. And one only.

Ben did not hesitate. He moved slowly forward, hand still ready by his gun if needed. He could feel the cell phone in his sweaty pocket, but that was definitely out of the question. And as he concentrated on not slipping a third time on the pine straw, he wondered what he would even say if he could make it to his cell phone.

Hey Lackey. Call all the dog catchers you can find in the phone book and send them out. We've got a few loose pups here in the woods.

He thought back to all the times he had teased his aunt's Chihuahua when he was younger. He would sling his Hot Wheels across the linoleum floor, trying to take out little Mimi's legs. The dog hated him. His aunt spanked him for it when she caught him in the act. Was this payback time?

He thought about all the dogs he had had since, as a boy and as a man. There had been only three total. Harvest had lasted from the time he was a small grunt up to his teenage years. Sister had lasted since his daughter's terrible two's until a random car smashed her one night and didn't bother to stop. They found her on the side of the road on the way to Ella's school. Wonderful way to start his daughter's school day. And the last one, they still had. His daughter was 12 now, and Blossom was a female Lab that ate anything not tied down. He had treated them all with love and respect.

But he had tortured Mimi. And as Ben hopped over the stream of water in the ditch that flanked the road, he fully expected Mimi to emerge from one of the dirty puddles in the road and leap for his throat.

But that did not happen.

A dog did emerge though from a tangle of gnarled roots that were hanging over the side of the ditch. The skin from what used to be its face was pulled back to reveal raw facial structure, and there was a hole in its head that looked like a firecracker had exploded inside its skull.

It walked to where the line of dogs ended and where Officer Braswell was now standing. It sat on its haunches about five feet in front of him. It was looking at him. It was not moving. He stared back, but only for a moment. He knew looking directly into a dogs gaze was an act of aggression. So he looked over at the ditch.

They stood in this uncomfortable way for over a minute, Ben wondering how awkward it would be for a driver to come barreling around the corner and see this in progress. That was when he began to feel it. Something fuzzy in his head. For a moment he was worried he would pass out and then this would all be over. But they had led him here for a reason. If they had wanted flesh, they could have taken that in the woods.

What then?

That's when it clicked. He was being made an offer of sorts. He was being measured. He wasn't completely sure, but it was getting darker by the minute, and he didn't want to be standing here when the sun was no longer there to cast shadows. So he stared back at the beast. He opened his mind to whatever possibilities might show themselves. His mind floated to the pistol, which didn't seem like an option right now. Then it floated to the driveway.

Mine.

It was as ephemeral as the blink of the lightning bugs he was beginning to see in the woods, but also as clear. There was some sort of communication here. In spite of wanting to just get out of the situation he was in, his curiosity pushed forward.

Why?

Mine.

It was obviously not up for discussion. And what the hell was he doing asking a dead canine why it was guarding a driveway? The dog still sat there, unflinching. He didn't know what it wanted. Or what to say.

Fine. He tried.

Nothing. His mind wandered to his daughter and that bothered him. He didn't want whatever this thing was being in his mind with his daughter in there. He was becoming paranoid. His thoughts returned to his cell...

And the dog immediately stood. Its paws started digging into rock and wet, orange clay, packed tight from years of use. The first little layer went quickly. And then the next layer and the next. He saw a rock the size of his hand fly out of the hole and strike a tree twenty or so feet behind the animal. It hit hard enough to remove a little bark. The dog stopped and moved back a little, but did not sit down.

The display of unnatural strength itself was enough to let Ben know that fighting wasn't an option. That if this beast wanted him dead, he would be. And quick. No, it wanted something else. And it hit him.

He had thought of the cell phone when the dog stood up. That was it. He reached slowly into his pants and pulled out the cell phone. Ben walked slowly forward, toward the dog and the hole. Then he carefully tossed the phone in the hole. He backed away as the dog moved forward and hiked its leg. What came out was, at first, the color of crude oil, followed by a clear white puss mixed with crimson. It made Ben wince.

Then the dog moved to the side. Ben moved forward without thinking. The deal was made. Negotiations were finished. He could not bring himself to look down into the hole as he crossed over it.

He walked a brisk walk, like the old people in the Oxford Mall. Not a run. He knew from being around dogs that when something ran, it was time to chase. He did not look back until he had gone around a bend. When he didn't see them in the road anymore, he broke out into a sprint.

After a half-mile, he slowed to a jog because his body forced him to do so. But coach would be proud. He wasn't going to stop for the world. He was leaving it all on the field.

16

Dan's head was reeling. He was so startled when he woke, he didn't know if he was still being attacked. His arms flew up to protect his face and his legs flew out, kicking wildly at the air. The bottle of Tequila, what little was left, rolled off of his leg (a little too much like it did in the dream, he thought) and hit the floor. A few bloop-bloop-bloops of alcohol gurgled from the mouth of the bottle, making a puddle on the hardwood floor. As his senses slowly returned, he spun around to look over the back of the couch. The pile of shit in front of the door was still there. No open windows. Looking down on the floor, there were no muddy paw prints, just his own dirty tracks.

He felt weak. Sluggish. Abnormally so. He had lost a lot of blood and drinking close to a fifth of liquor, a natural blood thinner, had probably not helped. He slumped back on the couch and peered out the window to his left. The light was almost gone. In a short time it would be completely dark. How far was the closest help? And could he make it to the boat house? Should he run for the water and try to swim around the lake until he saw someone's cabin lights on and start screaming for help? Tread water until dawn?

No. He would never make it and he knew it. The phone lines were gone. They had probably gnawed through them. What about power then? How long before they found a way to cut off the power? The thought of being alone in the woods, in complete darkness, with all of them surrounding him, was too much. He stared at the few glowing embers, surrounded by paper thin flakes of burnt-out gray.

He needed some sort of plan. Anything would do. But he couldn't just sit here and wait until they filed in, single file, and drug him outside for a midnight snack. He would have to fight back or find some way to draw outside attention.

He leaned forward to get up and throw a few more logs on the fire. There was something comforting in watching the fire. It was something that was still very much real and normal. It was a sort of anchor to reality. A reality that seemed to be slipping away from him at every turn.

When he had swirled around on the couch to check for monsters, his adrenaline had been pumping, fresh from the netherworld of dreams. But now his body protested. He felt as if rigor mortis had already set in. Normally, if he had been as drunk as he was now, he wouldn't have felt much of his body at all, but thanks to the severity of his wounds he could feel everything. The tightening of his muscles, as if he had slept the wrong way for a few weeks straight. The sharp pain in his ear, or what was left of it, like someone had shoved a sliver of glass just underneath the skin and was moving it to and fro, once every few minutes, just for fun. His leg, arm, thigh, and hand, all caked with blood, and the thigh still bleeding slightly. His scalp, and the way he could feel the air flowing over the open gash. And all of the above throbbing on and off with dull, restless pangs.

He moved deliberately and slowly and placed five more logs on the fire. He promised himself that by the time the fire had died down again, he would have a plan and do something. He didn't know what that something might be, but he would damn sure be doing it. He would not *go gentle into that good night.* That thought spurred another slideshow inside his paranoid head. One that no one likes to think about. His own death.

If he lost, what would happen to him? If he were to just walk outside right now and surrender, what would they do? Would they just rip him to shreds? A minute or two at the most and that would be it. And then who would find him? Karen? Her parents? And what would they all think about a man ripped to shreds in front of their cabin? No doubt the dogs would have disappeared back to the damn graveyard they crawled out of, or run out into the woods where no one would ever find them.

He thought of the neighbor's cat when he was younger. Nickel. Nickel used to bring them parts of mice that were half eaten as presents. And that's what he would be. He would be Karen's half-eaten present.

How fucking poetic.

He was almost feeling guilty, for just a split second. But then he thought about Charlie, maybe raising his leg and filling his mouth with one last stream of decomposing chemicals as Dan lay dying. And maybe Karen and some new boyfriend standing over his dead body at the funeral with a smirk.

"I told you so, asshole. I get the last word in. Not you."

That's what that smirk would be saying.

"Well fuck that," he said aloud. But not too loud because they might hear him. Then he thought about it again and said it louder.

"WELL FUCK THAT!"

This time, to make absolutely *sure* that they would hear him.

He listened intently for some kind of answer. An outside noise or Hell Hounds shattering through the front door. But there was only silence. No response.

The first thing he did was to go through any and all resources he had in the house: knives that could be tied to broom handles or chair legs and used as spears; glasses that could be broken and piled somewhere to cut feet or slow them down; electricity itself, which he had for now, that he could use if he flooded the floors of the cabin and then let them all in at once. Then he would drop a curling iron or something into the water and that would do something, wouldn't it? Food in the fridge. And even though it seemed silly, his mind was covering every angle, no matter how silly or bizarre. He could throw out some of the frozen chicken and pizza and maybe that would draw them away for a split second? There was lotion and shampoo that might make the floors slippery if they were chasing him. There was pots and pans, and HEY! That's it, armor. He could strap some of them to himself for armor. It would look silly as shit, but again, this wasn't going to turn out to be a beauty contest. This was brute survival.

There was always fire and things to set on fire. He thought about setting the whole cabin on fire and running for the boat launch. That would bring someone. But would he make it to the launch? There were other things he could set on fire and launch their way. Maybe making a path? There were the beds. He could light them on fire and throw them out of the screened in porch to make a line of fire or something. He had plenty of logs in the cabin, but rolling them down the hill outside the porch would just land them in the edge of the lake. If only it hadn't rained. He could have set the leaves and the whole damned forest on fire. California style. Fuck the other cabins and anybody downwind. There would be helicopters and news cameras and other people. And he had a really good feeling that if a bunch of other people were around, these beasts would make themselves scarce.

There was some bug sprays and poisons under the sink. He could make a small flamethrower with one of those. Useless. But keeping his mind free and in working order. He could use the rat poison on them. Someway. The forks as tiny spears. The glass in the windows as guillotines. And the hot poker for the fire as his sword.

Fire. Back to fire. He looked down at the alcohol he had left. It could have been used for a Molotov Cocktail. But now, even if he poured them into the same bottle, he would only have a half full bottle.

Idiot. You drunk fucking idiot. You drank up one of your resources.

Over the next thirty minutes, Dan affixed knives to broom handles he had broken over his knee. He duck taped forks and knives to some of the chair legs and laid them all in neat rows on the kitchen counter. He pulled out the paper towels and the toilet paper from the bathroom because they would burn easily, along with the clothes in the drawers and all the bath towels. The bigger burnables like the sheets and comforters came next.

Then the beds from the roll out. He plugged the drain in the bathtub and left the water running while he performed his rounds.

He took down pictures of Karen and family from the bedroom walls and set aside the Plexiglas. It could be sharpened on the sides and hurled like a razor sharp Frisbee of Death. He took the frozen pizza, chicken, and Michelina's to the bathtub and tossed them in. He laid a hair dryer on this bathroom sink but did not plug it in. Then he went back into the bathroom and plugged it in, making sure the cord would reach the floor. He admonished himself for being so safety conscious at a time like this. For good measure, he took a free standing floor heater, used during the winter months, and plugged it in but did not turn it on.

He went back to the pictures of Karen and family and spent a second or two ripping them to shreds before throwing them in the toilet. To hell with all of them and their damn cabin. He was using ripped bed sheets to tie a nine inch stainless steel frying pan to his leg when he heard the bath water spilling over the sides of the tub. He ran in, pots clanking, and turned it off. He grabbed all of the food from the tub.

The Michelina's containers were sopping as was the pizza box. He slid the food out as best he could and piled the partially defrosted chicken into the middle of the pizza. The other food was poured in the middle and hand-mixed with all the poison from under the sink. It was the blue pellet kind, and there were six boxes of it.

Should be plenty to kill a dead dog.

He laughed a humorless laugh to himself.

He grabbed a few pieces of flint from next to the fireplace and lit the ends, then carried them into the screened in porch and laid them on a fajita skillet. In case the lighter didn't work at the last moment. Then he took the two bottles of liquor and condensed them into one. He filled the other with the same amount of water. It was for testing his throw. This had to be perfect.

Another ten minutes and he had a pot strapped over his head with a piece of dishrag tied under his chin. A cartoonish version of a WWII soldier. Two thin baking pans covered his back and stomach, draped with cloth ties over his shoulders and crisscrossing at his chest like a feminine version of a Mexican outlaw. He had duct taped some spatulas and spoons around his arms, making it harder for their teeth to pierce the flesh. He had padded other areas of his body with potholders and tape for the same reason. He was aware that his neck was still naked and vulnerable, but couldn't think of anything to tape there without restricting his head movement or constricting his airflow. He left his feet and ankles bare for mobility.

He was ready, by God, for World War Three. If the Iron Chefs in Kitchen Stadium could see him now they would all be running for cover. He smiled. And then it quickly faded. Because the liquor was wearing off, and he was in pain, and it was time to just do this. Do or fucking die.

He turned off the porch light so he could see outside. With the lights out front, he could see the gravel area in front of the cabin quite well to the right. Nothing there. But the light seemed to stop abruptly at the edge of the forest, and what little speckles of light bled into the woods were swallowed quickly by a darkness one can only find in the deep woods. Slightly to his left and down past the rock and concrete steps, the single light, used mostly to clean fish by at night, lit only part of the boat house. It was just enough to aim at. And still there was no sign of a mutt corpse anywhere.

He took the knife and cut away a square swath of screen from the between the two by fours. Now there was room to throw. There was also a huge open area, though it was about seven feet off the ground on this side of the cabin. Unless they could climb walls or the poles underneath, he would be fine.

He would launch his attack, if you could call it that, from here. If that didn't work and they *could* climb walls, he would use the other flammables and finally make do with the knife-and-fork spears if it came to that. Then retreat back to the bathroom and try the electrocutions if he were forced. And after that, well... there was no after that. And he thought about that for a second. Him, standing on the bathroom sink, standing water everywhere, a lot of dead, or deader, dogs sizzling in ankle deep water, and Charlie still waiting patiently outside for him.

Enough. He grabbed the first bottle. Took very careful aim and visualized the toss in his head before launching it. Then he slung it.

He watched closely. He more heard than saw it. It crashed to the right, a bit short. But that was fine. That was why he had filled the bottle with the same amount of water and used it as a test.

He grabbed the next bottle and lit the rag. He took the same two steps forward and threw it a bit harder and a little more to the left. He stared at the boathouse and waited.

17

After the first two margaritas, Karen, Carol, and Hutz decided that a pitcher would be cheaper. So, they ended up getting two pitchers over the next two hours. They discussed the most recent events and then moved on to the whole whachu-been-up-to for the last nine years since Wellborn High. Turns out that Hutz had a degree in English. Karen and Carol were surprised, but tried not to let it show.

Hutz looked a lot like Cooter Brown from the Dukes of Hazzard. Not a bad-looking fellow, just a little backwoods with a slight 10 o'clock shadow at all times. You could tell he had sense. You could tell, after you shared a few back and forths with him, that he was definitely this side of Red, although you might not have been able to explain why. And that was fine with Jean Hutz.

Jean wasn't about to stick his nose in the air at anybody. There were no deep-seated cravings to break any class barriers or live in any certain neighborhoods. He'd started out poor as hell and worked his way towards a gradual betterment. And he remembered exactly where he came from, which was a little one-bedroom trailer on Six Mile Road that was also home to 3 brothers, 4 sisters, 3 dogs, and a goat. He hadn't had a date, not one to speak of anyway, in over two years. He was as happy as a lark to be jiving it up with these two beauties.

After jabbering on and on about everything under the sun for almost three hours, Jean Hutz got up from the table and excused himself for the fifth or sixth time. Karen and Carol watched him walk off and disappear into the back hallway. Then they looked at each other and smiled. Then they busted out laughing.

"What?" asked Karen.

Carol smiled a knowing smile.

"Whhhhhaaaat?" Karen asked again, herself smiling like a embezzler who's over the payroll department.

Carol laughed a silly tequila laugh and snorted a little when she did. They laughed harder. The waiter eventually came over and asked them if they needed anything else. He had been ready for them to scat an hour ago. As far as he was concerned, they were holding up tips for the evening.

"We'll take the check, please," Karen giggled.

More suppressed laughs. Then Carol asked, "and could you call us a taxi?"

The waiter nodded, forced a smile, and laid the check on the table.

Carol waited for the waiter to disappear and then slowed her giggles, her face turned into one of mock seriousness. She glanced at the bathroom hallway and then at the few tables near them with people close enough to hear.

Then she raised her eyebrows and whispered, "I will if you will."

Karen's mouth shot open. "You are bad. You are a bad, bad girl!"

More giggling. Hutz returned to the table and asked what he'd missed. That seemed to set the girls off, and there was more uncontrollable laughter. Hutz checked to make sure his zipper was up and there was no toilet paper on his shoe. He laughed along with them as they all got into the cab fifteen minutes later and headed back to Carol's.

18

Ben's side felt like someone had taken a large meat hook and slid it through his ribs, then tied a small car onto it for him to drag. His feet, especially his left foot, were soft, white pieces of soggy bread that someone was beating with a meat tenderizer. His winded, gasping-for-air breathing would have been embarrassing on the track. There wasn't a shred of cloth on his body that wasn't sweat drenched. Ben was fairly certain that if he were to sling his underwear against a wall right now that they would stick.

He had fallen twice. The first time was when he had first sprinted. He didn't know what had caused it then – maybe fear. Trying to run forward while you are looking behind you doesn't usually yield good results. The second time was a rock. His ankle wasn't twisted, thank God, but it had come pretty damn close. That second fall was only a few minutes ago, and had left him with another pain in the ankle to deal with. Not to mention a layer of skin shaved off his hand from attempting to catch himself. And the fall had knocked the breath out of him momentarily. But he was proud of himself. He had immediately jumped back up, both times, and started jogging again. He assessed his injuries on the run.

A lot had gone through Ben's mind on the way back to his cruiser. The first things where scenarios that would go down if these dead things suddenly emerged from the forest around him again. The lake down to his left had seemed like the only real choice he had. He figured the gun might pave his way if he was lucky, but he probably wouldn't make it anyway, so after about ten minutes of crack-head paranoia, he stopped worrying about surprise attacks and went on to other things.

It made sense on some level, although on what level he had no idea, that the dogs from the graveyard were the ones he had just tracked through the forest and then found. And it had been made very clear to him, through some sort of dead-dark canine telepathy that what lay down that driveway was not any of his business.

He shook his head, as if to shake out that eerie memory of the one that had told him, *Mine.*

We could tear you to pieces, but we're not. You just move on down the road and mind your own business – we'll handle ours.

But a dog didn't know words like 'mine', did they? And if it wasn't a dog standing there in front of him, then what the hell was it? Or maybe dogs do understand the concept of 'mine.' They're very territorial with their space and their food. Maybe. But someone, if so, would have to be translating.

He could see the newspaper ad now: *Dead animal translator needed for nights and weekends. Must love dogs.* He felt like he was losing his mind. And although his somewhat scientific mind wanted to, he no longer wished to go down a road where his mind was touching neurons with something that was dead. Something from the other side. He moved on again.

Next came the driveway and what lay at the end of it. From where he had been standing in the woods, and then the road, he couldn't quite see around the slight bend in the driveway. He wasn't sure whose cabin it was. He could find out from the old man that had let them in at the gate. But it had to be the guy in the SUV. Dan was his name. He suddenly felt very sorry for Dan. He wondered if the poor guy was being torn to shreds at this very moment. And then what? Would they go around the lake and kill everyone who happened to be out and about? He had to consider the safety of all the people in the immediate vicinity. But that didn't really make sense. If the pack he had encountered were bent on destruction and anarchy, they would have simply killed him on the spot. But they hadn't.

They let him walk. That in itself signified that they weren't just a murderous pack of the dead. They seemed to have a very specific purpose. And then there was the spooky way they had all collaborated in lining up in order, standing to attention when he went for his weapon, and sitting patiently for minutes on end while he and the head dog had their mind play. That wasn't anarchy. That was order. Discipline. An ordered, disciplined army of the dead with a very specific purpose.

Yes. He felt very sorry for Dan, whoever he was. What in the world do you have to do to deserve this kind of punishment right here on Earth. Kill a baby unicorn? It was eating at him. He was sworn to protect and serve. And he wasn't exactly protecting. He was running for his damn life.

He also had to decide what to tell Lackey and Wheels, who were probably becoming increasingly worried that Ben had been out of contact with them for almost forty minutes now. He looked like hell. And was bleeding. And would be out of breath from running. And why had he been running? Maybe because it was near dark, and he didn't want to get lost out here after dark?

He heard voices up ahead. As he got closer, he could make out what they were saying.

"Well I'm not going out there without any goddamn backup. And what the hell would we be able to see in the dark. Hell, we couldn't catch his trail in the daytime."

"All I'm saying is that we need to either call back at the station or . . . hell, I don't know. We need to do something. Surely he'd of called by now."

"This is just fucking ridiculous. I don't how in the hell we're supposed to . . . "

Ben slowed to a walk. They had noticed him down the road, but it was apparent they didn't know it was him when their hands went to their holsters. They had gotten themselves freaked out here in the gloaming.

Well, he thought, *you have no idea.*

He took a stab at yelling a short burst in between gasps for air.

"Me, Guys!"

Turns out that Wheels and Lackey were so glad to get the hell out the now black forest that they accepted his story without question. He had found nothing and jogged back to the car via the main in-road. And that was that.

As he followed the guys' taillights down the road he had just marathoned, he wondered if they would be stopped again at the driveway. He wondered if either one of the guys had their windows down. That might not be a good idea right now. His was up, with only a tiny crack so he could hear what was happening around the cruiser. He hated not knowing what was going on around him, especially in the woods. He wondered if other people were strange about that or if it was just him.

It only took about ten minutes, and they were coming around the bend that contained the entrance to the forbidden driveway. Ben tensed. He was looking everywhere. Down by the sides of his car. All around the other cruiser. Everywhere the lights were hitting in the woods ahead. And tapping the brakes every now and then to see if anything was behind him.

When Lackey's cruiser stopped abruptly in front of him, he almost rear-ended it. Ben had his twelve gauge on the seat next to him with the barrel in the floor, just in case. Now he reached for it. If either of them got out, he would have to get out too, and the more firepower the better. Then Lackey's head popped out of the window.

"Looks like it's down by the lake. We need to check it out or you think it's kids?"

Ben turned his head towards the lake and saw what had caused them to stop. Through the woods and about a fifth of a mile up ahead, somewhere down close to lakeside, something was ablaze.

*****

Dan couldn't quite see it hit, but he could hear it just the same. There was a very brief moment, less than a second, when nothing happened. To Dan, it seemed like eternity. Then the thing exploded into flames just like in the movies.

"Yeeahhh! HELL YEAH!" he screamed. He couldn't help himself. It was the only victory he had so far.

It hit the left walkway of the boat dock and the fire spread along the boards on the walk, up the first wooden pole that held a corner of the boathouse up, and into one of the Jon boats to the right of it. It seemed to be burning brighter by the second.

He watched.

He waited.

Dan's next hope was that the fire wouldn't peter out to nothing within a minute or two. The boathouse was made of 2 by 4's and 2 by 8's, but he was well aware that it took a little more than a flash fire to keep things burning.

He was looking down the slope and praying that the fire burned hot. Hotter than Hell itself. Burn, baby, burn. Light up the whole fucking lake and let's get everybody out here. When the fire trucks come, I'll hop in one and be gone, baby, gone.

After about twenty seconds, the fire did seem to lose a little of its original intensity, but it kept burning just the same. The splash of fire that had spilled over into the aluminum Jon boat had actually flamed up higher than the rest thanks to some pine straw that had piled itself into the front part of the boat. It was bright, but burned out quickly.

There was hope. Then there was movement below him on the slope. He reached over and grabbed two of his homemade spears, one in each hand. The shapes below him were a little to the left of the boathouse and very visible by the generous light of his little boathouse bonfire. There were about eight or nine shapes that slithered from the ground, seemingly from nowhere. Then they were on all fours and moved without haste into the black water below them, leaving tiny wakes that rippled in the firelight.

They were gone. Dan watched the water smooth completely back to glass.

"What the hell are you doing, you little bastards?"

The black shapes reemerged from the water, some directly next to the dock on the left and the others from under and around the Jon boat. It swayed gently in the water as they slinked up onto the boat dock. They immediately crawled onto the walkway and laid on the boards, sprawled like they were taking a cat nap in the sunshine. As they covered the fire with their sopping wet fur, tendrils of smoke suffused the night air. Then there was no light to see by again save the yellow one over the fish cleaning sink to the left of the boathouse.

Dan screamed. He wasn't aware of what he was screaming. He was just screaming. Screaming at the black shapes that had taken away the fire and his sliver of hope with it.

That had been Plan A, and there was no Plan B. He was standing on a screened-in porch, about 8 feet or so off the ground, and in front of a gaping hole in his defenses. Could they get in now? Hell, maybe they could have gotten in before. Maybe they were just playing with him for kicks. He looked over at the other flammables he had in his arsenal and realized how useless they were now. His homemade spears now seemed like toothpicks without purpose. He thought about the water in the tub. About flooding the whole cabin and then letting them in and frying them all. He thought once more about burning down the whole damn cabin, but this time from the inside out so they couldn't put it out in time. But in doing so, he would be forced at some point to make a run for the boathouse or die a witch's death.

It all seemed suddenly very useless. Very useless to try and escape. Very taxing and tiring just to imagine ways of getting out. All it did was muddle his senses and give him false hope. Why did it have to rain like it did? Why couldn't it have been as dry and as cheap as a bottle of Wal-Mart wine? His mind was beginning to shut down.

He backed away from the large hole in the screen, tiny-feeling spears still in hand, and then dropped them so he could pull the sliding door shut. He figured he would seal off the porch just in case.

In case of what, Danny boy? In case they can crawl up the wall and come in? If they can do that, Danny boy, then that little Plexiglas sliding door don't mean shit.

And he figured it might not. He figured he was just about done with this whole thing. He was tired. He was mentally wasted. He was fucked with no way out and he could feel it. Could feel it deep down in his bones. That by the end of the night, he would be zombie dog fodder.

Then he saw red and blue lights flashing outside.

19

Ben watched the taillights disappear ahead of him and was simultaneously happy and sad. Happy that Wheels and Lackey hadn't got dragged into this and sad because his only backup was gone. He wasn't exactly ecstatic about heading down the driveway that was not his.

Mine.

That had been made very clear. You could say that it had been part of a pact; an agreement. You go your way and I go mine – and no one has to get hurt. But now he was breaking that pact.

He rolled cautiously down the driveway and listened to the gravel crunch beneath the tires. His windows were rolled up, save a couple of inches at the top. He looked through the woods to his right and up the side of the small hill to his left, as well as he could see from his lights. He left off his side light for now and concentrated on what was around him. He had already made his mind up that he was not getting out of the car even if the whole cabin was ablaze.

As the cruiser rolled into the larger opening at the end of the driveway, he saw two cabins set across from one another. There were lights on in the one to the left. He made a wide turning arc to the right so he could see down the slope to the lake.

Nothing was on fire that he could see. Curious. Blazing one minute and nothing the next. He wondered if Dan was inside. He wondered if the dogs were finished with him yet. Ben pulled the cruiser back around in a figure eight so his window was only about twenty feet from the cabin front door, his front end facing the steps that ran down the slope. He flicked on his lights.

He was about to vlooop-vlooop the sirens when someone started screaming at him from the window next to the door.

"Hey! Don't get out of your car! Stay in your car! You're in danger!"

Ben could see the man he had stopped earlier, Dan, in the window. He was frantic.

"Hey! Can you hear me! Can you hear me! Don't get out! - your car! Stay in your car! Can you hear me!"

He hit the button and slid his window down just a fraction more, enough to talk back to Dan but not enough to get his face suddenly removed by one of the things he had seen earlier in the woods.

"What's your name?" Ben yelled back.

He knew the answer, but wanted to make sure.

"Dan. Daniel Stauberg. Look, you can't get out of your car. There's --"

Dan trailed off for a second. And what to say, really? There's a large pack of canine zombie hell-beasts that are trying to get me?

"There's a pack of wild dogs out there that attacked me earlier. So don't open your door, please."

"I'm not opening my door, don't worry."

Dan was watching the cop and noticed how he kept his window rolled up a little higher than was necessary. He also, now that Dan thought about it, had never made a move to get out of his car. That wasn't exactly like the cops. They were usually at your door knocking and asking questions. Since when did they sit in their cop cars and holler back and forth with people? He couldn't put his finger on why this bothered him, but it made him uneasy just the same.

"I need to get out of here but -"

Again, Dan trailed off for a second. But what? My car's in the lake. And then why is it in the lake, Mr. Stauberg?

"- my Jimmy broke down back on the road a ways, on the way in."

Ben looked around. No cars anywhere, here or next door at the other cabin. And he and the other cops had come the same way back from the graveyard that Dan had. They had seen no Jimmy. That meant he was lying. But it was obvious that he knew the dogs were out here.

Somewhere.

"I need to call the dog catcher?"

Why Ben suddenly felt the need to inject facetiousness into the conversation was beyond him, but he did it anyway. Maybe he wanted Dan to hurry up with a little more information so he could make a decision on his next move. But as he pondered what his next move would be, he came to the conclusion that his mind was already made up. He wasn't getting out of his car. That could lead to death. He wasn't letting Dan into his car. That would violate the pact. And mean possible death. And he wasn't calling in someone else who would be a clueless piece of meat the moment they stepped out of their car. His decision was made. He was just going through the motions.

But even with a decision made, curiosity still clouded his mind. He wanted to know why this was happening. What led to this madness? If there was some sort of path out there, some sort of cosmic, floating tunnel of Karma that was hidden just below the surface of this neck of the woods, Ben sure as hell wanted to make sure not to stumble upon it himself. And being a cop, he wanted to make sure that no one else was going to stray onto the path either. There were plenty of kids who sneak a half mile or so through the woods to land a few bream and bass through the week.

If this guy had dug up some sacred mound or something, he didn't want some kids traipsing unawares through the middle of it and ending up like poor Daniel here. Innocent until proven guilty. All he needed to do now was prove this guy guilty so he could get the hell out of here with a clear conscience.

"What? No. I mean – I just need you to hold on a minute so I can come out. Okay?"

Dan could finally see the light at the end of the tunnel. Come to think of it, he was simply elated there was even a tunnel now. A few minutes ago, there was nothing but despair and fear. Now there was a way out. There was a slice of reality and normalcy sitting outside in a cop car. And this warp in reality, this rift in space-time that had allowed Charlie to crawl up from whatever hellish abyss he came from, this shadowy existence was local to Dan. This was because...

Say it Dan. Say it.

...of what I did.

And it was out. Finally.

Dan the man had, for probably the second time in his life, owned up to something and taken responsibility for his wrongdoing.

Fine. Whatever.

Now let's move on. This madness affects my little world. They're after me. Fine. But these things with hollowed eye sockets and a lust for my flesh can't just follow me anywhere. I get in the car, and we drive to the middle of the city. I start a new life right in the middle of Atlanta or Birmingham. A few hundred Hell Hounds can't just creep around downtown Atlanta without being noticed. That would crack open a lot of other people's realities, not just mine. And they can't do that. Surely they can't. The whole world can't be a part of my madness.

The car. The city. Safety.

"Not going to happen."

Dan had moved from the window and started pulling a nailed in chair from the floor. What? He moved backed to the window.

"What?"

Ben responded, "I said, that's not going to happen."

Dan couldn't believe his ears. It made no sense. He spent a lot of his wild, college-drinking nights making sure that he stayed away from the back of cop cars. Now he was begging to be taken away in one, and the cop was telling him "no." Then he noticed the cop look back towards the driveway, and the woods.

He knows. He knows they're out there. He knows something. That's why he has the window rolled up and is yelling back and forth from the safety of his car. Son of a bitch. Then it settled in what was happening. The light at the end of the tunnel was getting smaller. And quickly.

Disbelief, denial, anger, grief, and fear. They came in such a quick succession that distinguishing one from the other was impossible. When you mix all the shades on the color wheel together, you get black. When you mix the tidal wave of emotions rocking Dan's tiny existence to and fro, you get blackness also. A black desperation so thick it drips like tar from your horrified thoughts and lands on your chest and spine, making it impossible to breath and even harder to move. Dan could see a crack forming in the Earth. It was filled with the howling rage of a thousand canine souls. A fiery chasm whose maw was ready to drag Dan down to the hottest parts of Hell where he could ponder the error of his ways for all eternity.

All Dan could muster was, "Why, sir?"

It was almost a whimper when it came out. Dan was not embarrassed. He was past that. He was past a lot of things now. He would do anything to be out in the real world again. Anything.

The cop just stared at him for a moment and then sighed deeply. He was thinking. Was that a good thing or a bad thing? Dan couldn't decide. He wanted to think it was a good thing. That he was thinking of rescuing Dan and putting an end to this lunacy. But now Dan was afraid of hope. Afraid of hope itself because hope had lied to him many times today. Hope was taunting him. Hope painted that picture that you see in the travel brochure. The one with the nice bedroom and the five-star dinning and the heated pool with all the hot chicks sunbathing, just waiting for you to rub oil on their tan bodies. But when you arrive at that hotel, the bedbugs are everywhere, the health score in the restaurant is a 72, the pool is ice cold in the middle of winter, and the only chicks at the pool are a couple of fat chatterboxes who talk a lot about family. Hope was a lying son of a bitch. Plain and simple.

So he shut down his mind and waited for an answer. No suppositions. Finally, the cop answered with a question.

"What did you do?"

Dan stared blankly.

He had already admitted to himself that all this bullshit was his fault. He had shit in his bed and now he had to lie in it. Now the cop wanted him to say it aloud. Why was it so damn hard to do that?

Maybe because saying it made it true. When it's locked inside your own thoughts, no one else has to know. You can justify and explain and lie to yourself and you know what? Your arguments don't even have to make much sense. You can lie to yourself every now and then. In fact, you can lie to yourself so much that you actually start to believe your own bullshit.

And that screwed up line of reasoning is fine and dandy in your own head. It's when someone who is reasonable starts asking you to explain yourself that your fragile tower of self-aggrandizing and ego-stroking propaganda falls like a house of cards in a monsoon. It's when you have to tell another your dirty little line of reasoning that you first begin to realize just how full of shit you really are. And Dan was knee deep in egotistical bullshit. He knew it. What he had done had felt really good after 14 beers. But now it didn't seem like such an accomplishment. There was nowhere left to run.

"I killed a dog, sir. My wife's... ex-wife's."

The cop looked out over the front of his cruiser for a second or two.

"Why?"

This was crazy. What the hell did it matter? He needs to just mind his own business and get me the hell out of here. Then a thought hit Dan. Maybe this dude has something to do with the whole thing. Maybe he's some kind of backwoods Shaman or something and instigated this whole thing. A cult or something. Who knows? It was a fleeting thought and didn't jive with the whole picture, but threw doubt into his mind nonetheless. Now he was wondering if he should even attempt to get in the car with the cop. But of course the answer was still a big fat YES. He had to get out of this cabin. This deathtrap. No matter what.

"Sir?"

The cop was looking exasperated. Not good.

He repeated, "Why?"

Dan was in a huge, glass interrogation chamber. Every eye was on him. This was his chance to confess. To cooperate maybe and, there's that lying bitch called "hope" again, lessen his sentence. And that brought on another strange thought. They were out there somewhere, not very far away. Could they hear him? Could they understand him? It didn't make sense, but he was past that, too. Screw sense. Screw anything that didn't lead to him escaping this gaping hellhole. Lessen the sentence.

"I cheated on my wife and she left me. I got really drunk and – and it was here that Dan felt himself slipping a little again. He wanted to say that the dog had bitten him and that he had retaliated, which would sound plausible, almost reasonable. But that would be leaving something out. And he didn't feel like that would be the thing to do right now – and shot my wife's dog with a pellet gun. He got off his run and attacked me and I got in my truck and ran him over. I killed him. That's it."

The cop sat listening. Then he looked up at Dan for a moment and continued to stare off into the distance. Dan wondered how it had sounded. It felt a little mechanical, but what the hell? He was under a lot of stress right now. He had confessed. Now it was time to cut a deal. He waited.

Dan heard something to his left and he jumped liked a scared schoolgirl. In his excitement and intermittent conversation with the cop, he had completely forgotten about the hole in the screen. There was something different. Water. Dripping from the painted two by four that ran underneath the hole in the screen. The image of the sopping wet dogs smothering the fire came to mind.

"Oh, my God. Oh, my God. No."

Ben sat in his car and thought hard about the situation. Sounded like the kid wasn't lying now. But so what? He purposely killed one of man's best friends. And then another moral dilemma crossed his mind. Should killing a dog bring about a death sentence? Ben believed in capital punishment. He believed that murderers and rapists and the like should hang in public. That it would save the taxpayers a load of cash and actually keep some people from committing the crimes in the first place.

But that was people to people crimes. Man vs. Man, as his old English teacher Mrs. Haught used to say. But this was Man vs. Dog. Did the same morals still apply? He knew you could go to jail for mistreating animals, but what would happen if you marched a puppy into a crowded mall and just shot it in front of a crowd of people? Where was the written law on that? Would they put you to death? What about in Texas? And this was what he was pondering again: if he left now, he would be the judge that was giving the death sentence to this man. Could he do that?

In reality though, it was another question. The question was whether you would put yourself in danger of getting killed if everyone in said mall suddenly attacked the guy who shot the dog, with the express intention of killing him and anybody that got in the goddamn way. The answer to that question was a little easier. Hell no. Dan brought it on. Good luck, buddy.

He looked up at Dan who was for some reason not paying any attention to him now.

"Son.... SON!"

Dan looked back at Ben. Ben looked solemnly at Dan.

"You need to make peace best you can, son. Good luck."

The window rolled up, the car went in gear, and Dan began screaming.

Ben rolled his cruiser back up the slight incline towards the main road and looked in his rearview mirror. He could see quick, flitting shadows behind him everywhere.

Hundreds.

20

Hutz was more excited than he had ever been. He had a hard time keeping himself from getting a woody on the way over to Carol's. They knew he was drunk. They all were. And now, about the time that it was time to call the night quits, the girls had invited him over. That was a very good sign.

He was thinking thoughts that he hadn't thought in years. Maybe a decade. About actually getting lucky. And how he was totally unprepared as far as protection. But then he was getting way ahead of himself. He shouldn't take all this the wrong way and then say something misleading that would make him look like a perverted jerk. And besides, if it came down to him getting lucky with one of the girls, he would find some way to make it happen. And didn't some girls in today's world bring their own protection?

He had heard giggling from Carol's room after the girls had disappeared into it about 10 minutes ago. He was finishing a Dos Equis when Karen and Carol walked out of the bedroom wearing what looked like little geisha girl night robes. They walked over to where he was standing and stood directly in front of him, smiling maliciously. His face was a blank slate. He was in awe. Today had begun like any other, but was sure as hell not going to end like any other.

Karen and Carol looked at each other, giggled under their breath, and both pulled the strings holding their robes together at the same time. As they slid apart, Hutz's mouth watered. He could see both sets of carpet. Both women were built. Karen even had the little vertical belly button going on, and Carol, oh Jesus, he had never really noticed how big Carol's tits really were. He didn't know where to start. He had never had two women at once and didn't know the protocol. So he stood up. He was already fully erect.

Carol moved her shoulders and the tiny robe dropped. She walked forward and grabbed his belt as he leaned down to kiss her. Carol immediately thrust her tongue in his mouth and began feeling around. The belt came off. He could feel Karen's hand now, grabbing his manhood through his pants. Then his tidy-whities were being pulled down along with his pants. He stepped out of his pants and underwear rather awkwardly, after finally removing his work boots.

Karen felt a little whorish at first. Sure, when in Rome. But she was still legally married. Then Dan popped into her mind and she tried to remove him. Couldn't get rid of the image of him with Charlie in the back of the Jimmy. The bastard.

In front of her, Carol pushed the now naked Hutz down on the couch. He was wild-eyed and that made her smile. Nice to know someone appreciated what he was getting. And there was his cock. It wasn't that much longer than Dan's, but it was longer still. By about two inches. And a little thicker too. She realized suddenly how wet she was.

Carol stepped up onto the couch and stood spread eagle with her bush right in Hutz's face. He immediately went to town. She kneeled down in front of Hutz and took his manhood in her mouth. It was so strange to have another man's junk in her mouth. But it felt good just the same. And he was hard as a rock. Her hand worked in tandem with her mouth, and she developed a rhythm. In less than two minutes, she could feel the head of his cock swelling. She sucked harder and faster. Then her mouth was full. She was so excited that she swallowed without even thinking about it, something she rarely did.

Hutz pulled his face from Carol's crotch for a second and apologized for the quick release.

"Don't be crazy," Karen said.

She turned around and sat down in his lap. She was dripping and he was still hard and so the head went right in. It took about fifteen or so strokes to take him in all the way. She began breathing heavily and losing some of the strength in her legs. She started another rhythm. She was bouncing up and down. Up and down. And with each bounce, she was bouncing Dan the Man right out of her head. In fact, it only took her about five minutes before her head cleared completely, and there was nothing but pleasure inside. She could hear the lapping sounds of Hutz's tongue in Carol's pussy behind her and to her surprise, that made her even more excited.

As her body began to shake out of control, she did something she hadn't done in almost four months. She smiled from ear to ear. And meant it.

21

Dan screamed and screamed out the window as the tail lights made their way out of the parking area. He looked at the sliding glass door and started ripping wood from the nails with his bare hands, jabbing himself several times and paying the puncture wounds no mind. The light at the end of the tunnel was going out completely. He couldn't let it go out. If he could just make it through the door in the next few seconds, he could run and jump on the back of the cruiser. And then what would the cop do? Get out and shoot him off? Drive like a demon and try to sling him off?

No. It would change the rules. Somehow it would work. Someway.

He slung the table to the side and yanked on the door, hard. Four, five, six, seven times. Harder and harder. The door was giving way and the last few shreds of two by fours and cabinet doors were giving way. The door was cracked now almost a foot. The police cruiser pulling up the driveway.

Dan screamed again.

"Noooooooooooo! Wait! Waaaiiiiitttt!"

He turned his body sideways and began forcing his way through the small slit. His clothes pulling away from his body. As he saw the last bit of red taillight disappear around the corner of the arching driveway, his foot that was outside on the stoop exploded in pain. There was a dog latched to it. First one. Then two. Then three on the leg as he forced his trapped and bedraggled body back into his prison. The pain was intense and he wondered, as he continued screaming, if their teeth were touching bone.

His left leg finally in, he slammed the door on the dogs' heads, over and over, screaming and screaming, like a maniac. His leg came free. He slammed the door and began throwing wood back at the door like it would stick to it on impact. His mind was on autopilot. He grabbed the tabletop and threw it against the door. But he threw it so hard, and it was so heavy, that it actually banged the door ajar slightly. Teeth gnashed through the tiny sliver of air.

He turned to look for one of his weapons. Anything. And what he saw beyond the sliding doors made his blood freeze solid in his trembling veins.

There were dogs coming through the hole, one after the other.

How?

And the ones that were through were scratching on the Plexiglas of the sliding doors like their pelts were on fire. Mud and grime from the lake below smeared in vertical streaks across the panes. Beyond this abstract painting from hell, there was a mass of movement that kept growing.

The first dog was about to break through the front door. The weight of the dogs pressing against the sliding doors made them vibrate violently. Dan was a statue of fear. He could not move.

This is the end.

A tear escaped his eye but he didn't notice.

This is my last night on Earth.

He remembered the bathwater. The electricity. He ran to the bathroom. Turned on the water in the tub all the way. The water in the sink. Had a thought. Ran to back to the living room/kitchen and turned on the sink in there also. Noticed the first dog was dragging its hind end through the door.

He ran to the bathroom. Grabbed the hair dryer. Ran down the short hall to the bedroom. Heard Plexiglas shatter. Slammed the door from the hallway shut and locked it. Slammed the door to the kitchen shut and locked it. Started throwing dressers and side tables at the doors. Throwing pictures also for no good reason. Stopped in the middle of the room again when he realized that he was screaming and couldn't stop.

He stood next to the bed, blow dryer in hand, and listened to the jowls and claws attack the doors to the bedroom. Again, no barking or growling. No guttural utterances from the other side of the door.

It was mind-numbing.

Torture.

He looked around the bedroom for weapons. He had pillaged them all already. They were in the kitchen and on the porch. Useless.

He looked around for an outlet. Found one next to the closet and plugged in the dryer. This would be the last thing. The last Hurrah.

Where should I lie? Where do I want them to find my body? Or will they consume all of me? Leave nothing but a bloody mess and a mystery?

Then he thought of fire again. Yes. Fire. What would it matter now? He would set the whole cabin on fire. Light the curtains and watch it burn. The smoke would overtake him in little time, and he wouldn't feel a thing after that. They could tear his body limb from limb, and it wouldn't matter. He would be out. Gone already.

He reached for the lighter in his pocket. Gone.

Hope. Gone.

Everything. Gone.

The hallway door jarred violently, as if one of the big ones, maybe a St. Bernard, had got a running start and tried to break it down. How long would it hold. Maybe five minutes if he was lucky? But what did that matter? Five minutes. Thirty minutes. Five hours. Either way, he was never leaving this room. Not whole.

He looked over at the kitchen door and saw, through some broken glass, a picture of Karen when she was younger. It was a basketball picture. Karen's two front teeth were missing. She was so young. Innocent. What was she doing now? Did she miss him? Would she miss him when he was gone?

Scratching. Scratching. Scratching. If only the scratching would stop.

He was screaming again.

"Stop! Stop! Stoooppp!"

He looked back to the hallway door and noticed water seeping into the carpet from under the door. Not gushing. Just seeping. Would they break through before the water rose high enough to drop the dryer and fry them all?

He ran over and started the dryer. Threw it under the comforter on the bed. Maybe he could start a fire after all. The muffled whirring of the dryer mixed with the cacophony of scraping and biting on wood to make a sickening symphony.

Dan looked behind him at the closet. He could hide there. The last stand. He opened the door. Looked around. Pulled out some summer clothes that smelled moldy and threw them on the bed. Raked a set of golf clubs out and threw them at the hallway door. What were clubs doing in a cabin in the woods?

Then he looked up and stopped.

An attic entrance.

Not the kind that pull down with a string and you then have to unhinge, but the small, useless square kind. But that was fine with him. The dryer stopped. He turned around and looked. Idiot! It's got a shut off for when it gets overheated. Stupid!

He pulled it out and threw it on the carpet to cool. Looked around. Still not much water. It was taking forever. He didn't have forever.

Dan ran to the other side of the bed and pushed the bed against the closet entrance. This would make it easier for him to get up through the small two by two foot square hole. Then he stopped. Walked over the bed and stepped into the closet. Pushed the bed back across the room. If it made it easier for him, the dogs might be able to get in also. Then he remembered. What does it matter? They were coming in through the hole in the screen. If they can shimmy up the wall, just what the hell difference does it make? It was that bitch hope again, rearing her ugly head. Teasing him with a way out.

Dan ran over to the hallway door and banged back on it with all his might. Over and over, screaming back at the other side, trying to cancel out madness with madness. He looked down at his hand and took notice for the first time of a large puncture wound near his thumb. It went almost an inch deep, he surmised. He looked down at his old wounds and the new ones he received recently while trying to get out of the cabin. He was a mass of mixed blood, some dried and crusty, and some shiny and wet. How much had he lost? A quart? Two?

He felt weak now. Walked back to the dryer and tried it. It turned on. He dropped it mechanically to the carpet. It could run until its little heart was content. If the water made it in, fine. If not, fine too.

He turned and looked up at the attic board. Jumping up a couple of times, he was able to knock the board to the side. He sullenly pushed the bed back over to the closet. He wasn't in enough shape to Jackie Chan it up the sides of the walls and push his way in. He heard the dryer going under the bed as he walked over it.

Positioning himself as best he could, he was able to reach up through the attic hole just slightly. He would have to jump all the way up to his shoulders and then catch himself with his arms, keeping them initially straight, in order to fit through.

The hall door came ajar. He hurried now.

First jump. Not high enough. Dan hit the floor of the closet much harder than he intended. Onto the bed again. Second jump. He aimed crooked and hit his head. Hard. Tears came involuntarily. He crouched in the closet for a moment, holding the top of his head. Instant headache. Things were moving by the door. They were coming.

Last chance. Third jump. Arms through. Arms out. And he caught. Hanging for a second, wondering if he had the strength to pull himself up. And then a familiar vice grip on his thigh, much too close to his privates. He hadn't the will left to scream. Dan kicked and kicked and whatever was below him held on. Something grabbed his shoe. He would have to stretch his legs out and place his feet on the closet walls in order to push himself up. That would leave his crotch exposed. No choice.

Place the legs. He could hear his pants rip and something hit the closet floor. The dog on his thigh had lost his grip. It was now or never. He pushed and used what little muscle was left to raise himself into the attic. Dan grabbed the piece of plywood cover and placed it back over the hole.

Pitch black darkness.

He sat on the board to stop them from crawling through and fished for his keys with the laser light and LED. They were in the Jimmy. In the lake. How silly. He wanted to roll over and take a nap. He was so tired. So, so tired. He felt around for something to sit on top of the board, but only felt the fluffy insulation in between the wooden joists.

In a way, he was proud of himself that he had made it this far. He wondered if anyone else would have already been eaten. He wondered if the water would come in before long and fry them all. There's still an out, after all. See. Hope, you old lying bitch.

Dan sat still for a few minutes and then felt the clawing and silent teething on the plywood under him. All he could do was sit like an Indian and wait. How much longer until daylight? As his eyes adjusted, he realized there was a small amount of light coming in through the octagonal vent at the other end of the attic. It was the outside light that sat next to the cabin and shone through the grate. Looking around, he could make out a slight shape of this and that, but nothing for certain. His eyes were adjusting slightly, but it was still black as night.

He stopped thinking. And listened. It had stopped. No more noise below him. No more banging on the plywood. He listened some more. He could hear the water he had turned on running its way through the pipes somewhere to his left in the darkness.

There was nothing for around two minutes.

A trick? Silence for a couple of hours and I poke my head out to get it taken off?

No. Something outside. Movement. Down below the grate. After a minute or two, he wanted to go look. Soft and whispery whatever it was. He wanted to go look, but was afraid to move from his position. As soon as he did, they would come barreling up through the hole. He listened some more. Moved slightly off the wood and placed his weight on his hands instead of his ass. Placed his ear on the board and listened.

Nothing.

But outside...

It was driving him mad. Madder anyway.

What the hell are they doing?

He placed his fingers on the edge of the wood and very delicately lifted it an inch or so, just enough to see below. Then he moved it more. There was nothing down there. He leaned to the side in order to see into the bedroom. Nothing. The dryer sitting there helpless. Still running. Still keeping the carpet good and warm and nothing more. Still no water in the room yet, not that he could see anyway.

He replaced the cover and made his way over to the grate, banging his head twice and placing his hand in something sticky once. What it was, he could not make out. It stuck to his hand but didn't smell like anything he knew. Who knew what the hell was in this attic? More damn golf clubs?

He sat by the grate and looked out below him. His eyes were showing him what it was, but his brain would not make sense of it.

At first, he thought it was one huge, four thousand pound Hell Hound, ready to ram the house and eat what's inside. Then he saw it for what it was. A mass of muddy death and fur. Almost eight feet high. Piled from the rise of the hill that the light sat on and stretching over to the house.

As he watched, another two or three of them ran up the pile and latched onto the fur and bones of another. Then a few more. The process repeated. It reminded him of the human teepees that cheerleaders build. He happened to look to his right and saw Charlie sitting patiently by the pile. He was waiting. King of the fucking hill.

Dan backed off. Made his way back to the opening to the closet and looked through, thinking that while they were doing that, he might be able to make it to the lake. The boat. Something.

But there were sentries on the bed now. Three of them. Large and dripping and staring right back up at him. Houston, we have a problem.

He slid the board back. So that was it. They hadn't climbed up the wall after all. They had engineered a real life dog pile.

He could hear Charlie's teeth on the aluminum. Heard the metal bend and give. He could see a little better now with more light coming in from the light outside. He could see Charlie move to the side of the wall and gradually slink along into the shadows as he moved his way. Couldn't hear him though. No. Even though all was quite now. As if the forest creatures and the wind itself had all agreed to take a moment of silence for this special event. He couldn't hear a thing in the attic. All quiet on the western front.

He turned his head in the direction that Charlie would be coming from and stared into the darkness. Waiting.

He waited for a full two minutes. He stared ahead. Mind blank. Waiting.

After what seemed like an eternity, Dan could make out a shape not five inches from his face. Dan cried again. After crying for a full minute, the waiting got to him, and he started sobbing like a three-year-old stung by a switch, shaking and trying to catch his breath. One more plea. He really, really meant it this time.

"Ple-he-he-ease. I'm so-ha-rar-ree. I'm sor-ry, Cha-har-lie. I'm so sor-ry Charlie."

And he really did mean it this time. He sat a bit longer crying. Staring wide-eyed into the darkness like people do. After a few more minutes, Dan's sobbing subsided a little, and Charlie's shadow moved away from Dan's face.

Maybe. Just maybe

Oh, hope.

You old bitch.